THICK GIRLS POLE

PEACHES & POLE BOOK ONE

TINA GALLAGHER

GALSALLA PRESS

Thick Girls Pole: Peaches & Pole Series Book One

By: Tina Gallagher

Published by Galsalla Press

Copyright © 2022

Cover Design: Qamber Designs & Emporium

Editor: Jeannine Luby

For Meghan...of all the things pole fitness has given me, I'm most grateful for your friendship. It's an honor being your "pole mom."

CHAPTER 1

Keera

"How did you survive for so long without sex?"

Anjannette looked up and blinked, then raised her right brow.

"When I asked if there was anything else we need to discuss, my sex life isn't what I had in mind."

"I definitely don't want to talk about what your sex life is like now. That would only make my celibacy seem worse, even if it is voluntary. I want to talk about your dry years prior to Leo." I smirked and bobbed my eyebrows. "Pun totally intended."

"I guess we're done with business." She closed her laptop and rested her elbows on the table. "But thankfully everything looks great and it seems like the open house is all set. You don't need me here at all."

"You know that's not true. You're the heart and soul of this place. Everyone misses you when you're gone."

After dedicating herself to the Peaches & Pole for the

better part of three years, Anjannette met and fell in love with Leo Marakis, All-Star catcher for the Carolina Waves. When I got downsized by corporate America, she brought me on as a partner, which was definitely a win-win. It gave me enough of a bump in income so I didn't need to find another job and also allowed her the flexibility to travel with Leo throughout the baseball season.

"And don't think you're going to distract me from my question."

She took in a deep breath and let it out on a dramatic sigh.

"All right. What do you want to know?"

"Just what I asked. How did you survive without sex for so long?"

"I remember giving my toys a workout for six months or so, but after that, I just didn't crave it anymore. Plus I was putting all my energy into this place, so that helped shift my focus," she said. "How long has it been?"

"Five months, one week, and three days."

"That's very specific."

"I could probably tell you the hours and minutes too if I really thought about it," I said. "And I've been giving my toys a workout, but they're just not doing it for me anymore. It's much more enjoyable when someone else does the work. Know what I mean?"

"Yeah." Anjannette's mouth curled into a sappy, smitten, and super-satisfied smile. "I know *exactly* what you mean."

"Oh-kay."

The chair scraped against the floor as I pushed back from the table and stood.

"What's wrong?"

"You know that I'm really happy for you, but I'm so freaking jealous right now. I'm ready to jump out of my skin I'm so horny, and you and Leo are fucking like bunnies."

Her eyes widened and she stared at me for a few heartbeats before flashing that satisfied smile again and dramatically nodding her head.

"Yeah we are."

I burst out laughing then leaned down and pulled her into a hug.

"I truly am happy for you." Shifting back, I squeezed her shoulders then let her go and straightened. "I'm just cranky." I stuck my bottom lip out and used my best whiny voice to add, "I really like sex."

Anjannette stood and leaned her hip against the desk.

"The only thing I can suggest is what really helped me. Focus on why you gave it up in the first place."

She raised her voice on the last two words of that sentence turning it into a question. I never really told her why I decided to take a break from men. Initially, I didn't have a concrete answer, it was just something I felt I needed to do. It's a little more clear now, but knowing doesn't make it any easier.

"You're partly to blame for my celibate state."

"Me?" She placed her hand on her chest. "What did I do?"

"You started a healthy relationship with your hottie ballplayer that made me want more than random hookups with dick band-aids. Plus those hookups got old. I realized I was just going through the motions and it became more like a bad habit than something I enjoyed."

Anjannette's image blurred and I blinked several times to push back the tears.

"You okay?"

"Yeah." I dabbed at my eyes. "You know I've never been a

crier, but lack of sex must have my hormones all scrambled because the past couple months, the waterworks are never too far off. Sappy movies and sweet commercials have me tearing up and I even got emotional last week after my class perfectly executed a new routine."

"Have you talked to Dr. Green about it?"

When I decided that I finally wanted to deal with some emotional baggage, Anjannette recommended her therapist, Dr. Green. *Dr. Rachel Green.* It's a struggle for me not to make a *Friends* reference every time I'm with her.

"Yeah, she said that crying is an excellent way of releasing emotions and processing difficult situations." I used air quotes to highlight my therapist's words. "I still don't like it and can't help but wonder if it's worth it. Like seriously, why am I doing this anyway?"

"Change is hard, but it'll be worth it. Honestly, I don't think things would have worked out with Leo if I hadn't focused on myself before we met. I wouldn't have been capable of having a healthy relationship." She squeezed my hand. "You went through a lot with Brian but when you guys broke up, you never really took time to deal with it. Which is exactly what I did for years. I moved from guy to guy, making the same stupid mistakes. The thing is, eventually all that stuff you ignore builds up and tarnishes everything."

My issues didn't start with Brian, but he definitely highlighted all my insecurities. I've always been a bigger girl and I'd be lying if I said that didn't bother me. Pole dance helped me appreciate my body for its strength and even made me feel sexy, but in the back of my mind, I always wish I was smaller.

"When we first got together, Brian said he loved my curves, but once he lost some weight and got obsessed with fitness, the insults started. He complained about what I ate and wore, especially if we were with his Crossfit friends." I snort-laughed. "The sad part is, if I hadn't found out he was cheating, I'd probably still be with him."

"Yeah, same with Travis and me," she said. "And when Dr. Green pointed out my bad pattern and suggested I take a break from men, I hated the idea. Thankfully I'm stubborn and decided to do it just to prove her wrong, because she was totally right."

"I'll admit I thought you were crazy. I couldn't even imagine going cold turkey like that."

"So what changed?"

"Brian isn't the first guy I've dated who ended up commenting on my weight." I blinked away tears as I looked around the studio before meeting her gaze again, then shrugged. "One-night stands with random guys kept me safe from that. Plus the sex was good. In the beginning anyway. I just went through the motions with the last few. But that's not how I want to live my life going forward. I want to spend it with someone who loves me for me and doesn't care about the size of my body."

She pushed away from the table and pulled me into a hug.

"I'm so happy you decided to make a change." Releasing me, she added, "You're beautiful inside and out and someday you'll meet a man who recognizes that and will treat you like the goddess you are."

"Say that louder for the universe to hear."

SIMON

· · ·

My phone buzzed and I cringed when I saw my sister's face pop up on the screen. I thought about ignoring the call, but that would only delay the inevitable.

"How's my favorite sister today?"

"I'm your *only* sister and I'm pissed," she said, then added, "At you." As if there was any question.

No use pretending I don't know what she's talking about.

"Shannon, I took Andi out to dinner then dropped her off at the hotel. I don't know what else you expected to happen."

"I *expected* you to give the date a chance. She said you barely spoke and when you did, you gave one- or two-word answers."

"I did give it a chance," I said.

"By sitting there silent and just nodding like an idiot?"

I closed my laptop and shifted forward to set it on the coffee table. Resting my elbows on my knees, I told her my side of the story.

"I got a few words in at the beginning, but once I asked about her job, she barely stopped talking to breathe. So instead of interrupting, I just listened and nodded."

"It couldn't have been that bad."

"Do you want me to tell you about the designers she's worked with, items of clothing she's worn, and which makeup she prefers?" That question was met with silence so I'm guessing Shannon has experienced similar conversations with Andi. But since she's being quiet, I figured I'd drive my point home. "I could also tell you which photographers are her favorite, although by that point, I was only half listening so I won't be as detailed."

I heard a long sigh and sat back waiting for my sister to speak.

"Did you like her at all?"

"I didn't *dislike* her, but she's not someone I'd want to date."

"Just because of the talking?"

"Honestly, we don't have anything in common."

"Okay, no Andi," she said. "But I do have someone else in mind that I think you'll connect with better."

My sister is a makeup artist for some of the most prestigious photographers in Manhattan so she has a never-ending supply of beautiful women at her disposal.

"I appreciate the thought, but I'm good. Besides, people will start avoiding you if they think you're going to hit them up to go on a date with your nerdy brother."

"My friends think you're adorable and would jump at the chance to date you."

"I seriously doubt that."

"Why not? Nerds are in you know," she added with a chuckle.

Penny and Leonard end up together on *The Big Bang Theory,* but chances are, they'd crash and burn in the real world. There are exceptions of course, like my parents, but my experience has taught me that my sister's friends and I just aren't a good fit.

"We're too different. Your friends are like you. None of them would be content doing the low-key things I enjoy and I definitely don't fit in their world."

"Relationships are about compromise. Look at mom and dad. They're as opposite as can be and still make it work."

"Mom and dad are the exception," I said. "And besides having nothing in common with your friends, I live in Scranton and they're either in Manhattan or travel all the time. Andi's photo shoot in the Poconos is the only reason we managed to go out."

"I have friends closer to Scranton."

I took off my glasses and rubbed my eyes.

"Shannon, please find another project."

"You and Zoe broke up almost two years ago and aside from the women I've set you up with, you haven't had a date."

"And I'm okay with that."

"Simon, you're a great guy with a lot to offer. I know you'd like to be in a relationship, you just need to meet the right girl. That's not going to happen if you're hiding at mom and dad's playing video games with Andrew and Archer."

My sister and I may be twins, but we're total opposites, in looks, interests, and lifestyle. Where she's like our outgoing, popular father, I take after our more reserved mother. Shannon has made it her life's mission to get me out from behind my computer and make sure I don't end up living in our parents' basement.

"You know I only moved back home because mom and dad took off on their tour of the country. Once they come back, I'll get my own place."

After Zoe and I broke up, I moved into a studio apartment because it was fully furnished and available, but ended up living there longer than I should have. My lease was up, so when mom and dad bought an RV and planned their epic journey, I decided to move back home. Staying here will give me time to find something new and would also make keeping an eye on their house easier. It seems like a win-win to me. Shannon thinks I'm going to stagnate here.

"We'll see."

I swear I heard her eyes roll through the phone line.

"Shan, I went away to college then moved in with Zoe a couple years after I graduated. You make it seem like I've been a hermit."

"Not a hermit exactly. I mean, you go to work and hang out with your friends once in a while," she said. "But let's be honest, you spend more time with your dolls than you do with people."

"They're not dolls, they're collectibles. And I don't play with them. They're on display."

"Okay Andy," she said, referring to Steve Carell's character in *The 40-Year-Old Virgin*.

"On that note, I'm gonna say goodbye."

Her answering laugh should have aggravated me, but for some reason, it made me smile.

"Talk to you later, big brother."

I disconnected the call and picked up my computer, but the game I'd been playing before Shannon called wasn't keeping my attention anymore. Something my sister said kept running through my head. I would like to be in a relationship and if I'm being honest with myself, I know who I want to be in one with. Opening a new browser, I signed onto Facebook and typed in her name.

Keera Jordan.

We worked together for almost a decade before her position was downsized last year. I had a crush on her from day one, but she was dating then engaged. Plus I was with Zoe part of that time. Even if those things weren't true, I'm not sure I would have asked her out. Besides the fact we worked together, we were friends. If things didn't work out or she wasn't interested, that friendship would have been messed up and I'd have to face her every day.

But now that wouldn't be the case. My ego would be bruised if she turned me down, but I'd live.

I scrolled through her feed, which was mostly pictures of classes at the pole dance studio she's working at now. Then something caught my eye. They're having an open house at the studio next weekend. Before I could second-guess myself, I grabbed my phone and dialed Shannon.

"Do you have plans next weekend?" I asked as soon as she answered.

"Nothing that can't be blown off or changed. Why?"

"There's an open house at Keera's pole studio Saturday and I was hoping–"

"I'll be home Friday night."

Sometimes it's not so bad having a pain-in-the-ass sister.

CHAPTER 2

Keera

"You're home on a Friday night again?"

I looked over at Granny Vi as she shut the front door behind her.

"Yeah, tomorrow is the open house so I wanted to get to sleep early. It's going to be a long day."

"That makes sense." She nodded and sat in the recliner across from me. "But what's your excuse for being glued to that couch every weekend for the past five months?"

"What do you mean? I've gone out."

"You've gone to the studio and maybe to eat with your friends, but you haven't gone *out* out. Not like you used to, all dressed up."

She's not wrong, so I just shrugged. Looking down I traced the sugar skull pattern on my leggings.

"It wouldn't kill you to put on something besides leggings, swipe on some lipstick, and maybe go on a date," she said. "I'm not saying I want you out there shtupping random men like you did after you broke up with Brian the buffoon, but I think it's time you put yourself out there again."

I nearly gave myself whiplash when I jerked my head up to look at her.

"Granny Vi! You can't say stuff like that."

"Why not? I'm 3.8% Ashkenazi Jew, you know."

"I'm aware. And don't think I don't regret the day I got you a DNA test for Christmas last year." She crossed her arms over her chest and glared at me with what I like to call her defiant look. "I don't care if you say *shtupping* or any of your other new-found Yiddish words. Just please don't use *any* word that means sex in reference to me."

"Why not?"

"It's icky."

"I didn't ask for details."

"Can we please change the subject?"

"How did my granddaughter end up being such a prude?"

"I'm not a prude. I just don't want to discuss my sex life with my grandmother."

Or God forbid, hear about hers. The fact that she and my grandfather had sex on the kitchen island on the regular unfortunately lives in my brain. She casually dropped that particular bomb one night while we were watching a movie and the couple was doing it on the kitchen counter. My poor grandfather probably rolls in his grave with some of the stuff she shares.

She's always been super open about things. Her belief is that if someone asks a question...even a child...they deserve an honest answer. Which is how I learned the truth about Santa Claus at eight years old and some facts of life not long after that.

"So what's going on? You broke up with Brian the moron, then were out every night painting the town, and now nothing for months. Are you depressed?"

"No, I'm just trying to figure out some things and I think I'm better off alone right now."

"Just don't let Brian linger in your head. You know I didn't like him at the start and he just got worse as time went on. He always seemed like he was looking for the next best thing. What he didn't understand is that *you* are the best thing and he should have worshipped you instead of being such a shit."

I blinked back tears.

"Thanks Granny Vi."

"He definitely suffered from small-man syndrome." She raised her brows. "And since the man is 6'5", I'm assuming the size deficiency is in his schmeckle."

I burst out laughing, both from the look on her face and her words.

She's not totally wrong. Brian is barely average, but since he's such a big guy, his dick looks smaller than it is, which definitely bothered him.

"You're not denying my words, so I must be right. I can always tell what a man's working with."

"My grandmother, the penis psychic."

"It's definitely a gift. Feel free to consult me before you decide to get involved with someone again."

"Maybe I'll switch to women, then I won't have to worry about it."

"You think women are easier to deal with than men?"

Her accompanying snort told me her opinion of that.

"I don't know what the answer is," I said. "Maybe I'll just move to a remote island and live alone."

"There's no reason to be dramatic. You've got a lot to offer. All you need to do is find the right guy."

"I'd have better luck finding a unicorn."

"Decent men are out there, you just need to be open to them instead of focusing on the same toxic types like you've been doing."

"What are you talking about?"

"You know you have a type. Tall and muscular with a fragile ego."

"I don't know about that last part, but I do like bigger guys."

Mostly because they make me feel smaller. But I didn't say that out loud because it would lead to a whole other conversation and I'm getting tired.

"If that last part wasn't true, they wouldn't need to put you down to make themselves feel better."

I'm paying Dr. Green a good chunk of change every week and she basically told me the same thing. Maybe it's time I start listening.

Simon

"So what's the plan for tomorrow?" Shannon asked, then shoved a handful of popcorn into her mouth.

I looked over at my sister curled up on the other end of the sectional couch. She arrived around dinnertime and instead of heading out with friends like I thought she would, we're spending Friday night watching *Deadpool*. In recent years, we've found some common ground with my "nerdy movies" since some of her favorite actors now star in them.

"Beyond going to the open house and talking to Keera, nothing. What more is there?"

Shifting into more of a sitting position, she crossed her legs and set the popcorn bowl in her lap.

"Simon, she's probably going to be busy. You'll need a plan of attack so you can get in, make your offer, and get out."

"You make it sound like I'm going to war."

"Not war exactly, more like playing a game." She smirked. "You spend enough of your time doing that, so I shouldn't have to explain the need to strategize."

"Keera and I are friends so it's not like I'll be going in cold. I'm just going to ask her if she wants to go out to dinner."

"Just be sure to make it clear you're asking her out on a date so you don't get friend-zoned."

"How about I just ask her out and take it from there?"

She held up three fingers in the shape of a W, our preteen sign language for *whatever*. Why is it when Shannon and I are together for more than five minutes we revert back to juvenile behavior?

We watched the movie in silence for a few scenes and I thought she was letting the whole subject drop. History should have taught me that wouldn't be the case.

"Are you nervous?"

"No." She looked at me, brows raised. "Shan, I'm not a tween asking a girl to the school dance."

"I just don't want you to get there and choke."

"I'm not gonna choke."

Shannon didn't look convinced, but instead of responding, she shrugged and shifted her attention back to the movie. I did the same and groaned when I realized we're at the sex holiday montage scene set to the song "Calendar Girl." It's not overly graphic, but also not something I want to watch with my sister either.

Grabbing my phone from the end table, I checked my stock portfolio then scrolled social media. Once the music changed, I knew it was safe to look at the TV again. Unfortunately, Shannon's words kept echoing through my head and I couldn't focus on the movie.

Instead, I mentally rehearsed what I'd say to Keera, how I'd ask her out, but it all sounded lame. Then again, nothing is as lame as a thirty-two-year-old man sitting home on a Friday night practicing how to ask a girl out.

Leaning back, I propped my feet up on the coffee table, reminding myself that there's really nothing to be stressed about. After all, Keera is a friend. All I'm doing is asking her on a date to see if there's potential for us to be something more.

Even though I didn't totally believe myself, I managed to relax enough to focus on the movie.

CHAPTER 3

Keera

"This turnout is crazy," I said to Anjannette.

"Those last few women saw your social media posts but everyone else I've spoken to heard about this through word of mouth." She looked around the full room. "Offering current students a discount if they bring friends was a great idea."

"Our students are our best promo for sure."

I glanced at the clock.

"It's time for our first demo. You ready?"

"Are you sure you don't want to do it?"

"Positive. This one's all yours."

Anjannette clapped her hands together.

"Can I have your attention?"

Eventually everyone stopped talking and shifted their attention to Anjannette. I looked around while she thanked everyone for coming and explained what we have planned for the day. The room is pretty much an even split between current and potential students right now. I'm excited to see who comes through the door in the next few hours.

"Okay, we have ten poles," Anjannette said. "Who wants to learn the short dance I put together?"

Surprisingly, seven women immediately stepped up and three current students took the remaining poles. We didn't have to encourage or twist arms or beg. That's a pretty good start to the day.

Anjannette stood at the instructor's pole and demonstrated some basic moves. At first the new ladies were timid, but once she had them doing a fireman spin down to the floor, most got into it.

After perfecting the moves, and running through the routine a couple times, Anjannette said, "You all look awesome. Let's put it to music. Anyone have a song request?"

Surprisingly, someone did.

I walked over to the iPad and found "I Feel Like I'm Drowning" by Two Feet on the playlist. The women stood ready at their poles and when the first strains of the song filled the studio, they started the routine by walking around their poles. I couldn't help but notice their moves were much more poised than when they started. And not just confident, sexy.

They did a step around then a pirouette that settled into a backbend with their right leg popped in the air. The other attendees clapped, cat-called, and cheered, and one even gave an impressive whistle.

After straightening, each executed a perfect fireman spin then slowly slid down to the floor. Keeping their head and shoulders down, they lifted their butts to "booty up" then did a hair flip as they straightened. With right hands high on the pole, they crossed the left ankle over right to end the dance.

"That was amazing," Anjannette yelled over the applause of the other attendees.

"You ladies were perfect," I said as I lowered the music.

The women who'd just danced were beaming as they looked more confident and self-assured than when they walked in. This is what I love about pole dance. It's so empowering and it makes people happy.

I absorbed the energy vibrating through the room as I greeted new arrivals. Making my way over to the information table, I checked to see if Sophie and Eve needed help.

"I was just going to flag you down," Sophie said. "The beginner's bootcamp is full, but I've started a waitlist. Do you have any idea when you're scheduling another so I can let people know?"

"No." I glanced over my shoulder at Anjannette as she approached and relayed Sophie's words. "Since this is the first time we're offering it, we figured we'd see how it went and then decide if we're going to do another."

"I'd say it's going well," Eve said with a chuckle.

"Take contact information from anyone else who's interested and tell them we'll reach out and let them know our plans for another beginner series within the week," Anjannette said.

Both Sophie and Eve nodded then turned their attention to a group of women who approached the table.

"This is all so amazing." Anjannette looked around the room. "I thought people would just stop in for a few minutes, but it doesn't seem like anyone is leaving," she said, looking over at the doorway as some more people shuffled in. "Isn't that your friend Simon?"

I shifted my eyes toward where she was pointing and

saw Simon talking to a beautiful woman over near the doorway. She stood a couple inches taller than him and her thick brown hair fell across her flawless skin as she bent her head to say something to him.

"Who's that woman he's with?"

"His girlfriend, I guess."

I hadn't heard that he was dating anyone, but it's been a while since I've spoken to him, or anyone from my previous job for that matter. We went to happy hour regularly when I was first let go, but those became more sporadic as time went on. It's been a few months since we last went out.

The woman said something to him and he shook his head then looked over and caught me watching. Smiling, he raised his hand in an awkward wave.

"With the way he's looking at you, the way he's *always* looked at you, I feel bad for that woman if she is his girlfriend."

I waved back.

"You're insane."

Anjannette rolled her eyes.

"You seriously don't see it?"

I returned her eye roll and shook my head then walked across the room toward Simon.

Simon

Shannon took a few steps away from me as Keera walked in our direction.

"Hey stranger, it's so good to see you," Keera said. "Although I have to say, I'm surprised to see you *here*."

"When I saw you were having an open house, I figured I'd come check the place out since I've heard so much about it."

Her eyes shifted to Shannon who was standing a few feet away. I was about to call her over to introduce them when a woman approached and asked Keera a question. She excused herself and my gaze tracked her as she followed the woman to the information table.

Shannon appeared back at my side and nudged me with her elbow. When I didn't respond to that, she pinched my side.

"Stop," I whispered.

"You need to cut to the chase and ask. She's busy and people are going to keep interrupting."

"We literally had just enough time to say hello." I looked around. "But you're right, she is busy. Maybe this isn't a good idea. I can just call or text her."

"You are *not* texting to ask her out. Have a little class. You're not a frat boy making a booty call on a Saturday night."

"I'll call her then. This was a stupid idea. Of course she's busy."

"It wasn't stupid. You got this. Just take a deep breath and relax."

Normally it annoys me when Shannon says stuff like that, but right now, I'm grateful she's here. I've been interested in Keera for a long time, but never thought I'd have the opportunity to ask her out. Last night, I really thought I had this all under control, but now my palms are sweaty and I feel like someone punched me in the gut.

"Remember what you said last night," Shannon said. "You don't have anything to lose. You guys don't work together anymore, so it's not like you'll have to see her every day."

I did say that and it sounded so logical but now the words aren't offering much comfort. Because if I don't have to worry about seeing her every day, it means she turned me down.

"Shhh, she's coming back," I said.

"I wasn't saying anything."

"Sorry about that," Keera said.

"No problem. I know you're busy. Before I forget my manners, this is my sister Shannon." I shifted my gaze between them. "Shannon, this is Keera Jordan. We worked together at Wilder."

"It's so nice to meet you," Shannon said.

Keera's eyes widened as they shook hands, a typical reaction when people find out we're siblings. The reaction intensifies when I mention we're twins. We barely look like we're related.

"Simon mentioned he had a sister, but he didn't tell me you're gorgeous. I'm so jealous of your hair." She wrinkled her nose. "And your skin. It's flawless."

"I'm a makeup artist so trust me when I tell you the skin is all smoke and mirrors. And my hair is nothing compared to yours."

Keera pushed her thick brown hair over her shoulder.

"It's the one thing I can thank genetics for."

I'd half expected Shannon to make some snarky comment about my ginger hair, but she didn't. I guess she really is trying to help me out here.

"Shannon is in town this weekend and when I mentioned the open house, we decided to come check out the studio."

"I'm so glad you did." Keera glanced around the full

room. "It's so good seeing you. I wish I had more time to get caught up, but it's so crazy here. Not that I'm complaining. I was afraid we'd be sitting here in an empty room."

"That would never happen. You've worked so hard here, it's bound to be successful."

"This is a labor of love. Sometimes I still can't believe it's what I do for a living."

"It's not the same at the office without you, but I'm happy for you."

"I do miss the people at Wilder. Especially you." She glanced at the clock on the far wall.

"Can you guys stick around? We're doing routines on the hour and I'm leading the next one. But I'd love to chat some more."

Shannon and I talked about this last night. When I planned on coming today, I figured we'd hang out for a while, but my sister said I needed to get in, ask my question, and get out. Hopefully with future plans in place with Keera.

"No, we have to go," I said. "We just wanted to stop in, check out the studio, and say hi."

"We'll all have to get together," Keera said. "It really has been too long."

My sister cleared her throat next to me and I shifted my eyes in her direction.

"I'm going to go get some water." she said. "It was so nice to meet you, Keera."

"You too."

Shannon gave me a thumb's up as she walked across the room. Thankfully she was behind Keera's back so there was no chance of her seeing.

"Actually, I was wondering if you're free Wednesday night."

I'd initially planned on asking her out for Friday or Saturday, you know, typical date nights. But Shannon talked me out of it. She said Wednesday is less threatening for a first date. Plus, if things go well, there's the option to have a second date on the weekend.

"Are you planning a happy hour?"

"Not really." I looked down at the floor and rubbed the back of my neck. "I mean no," I said as I met her gaze again. "I was wondering if you'd like to go out to dinner. With me," I added, just in case my intentions weren't clear.

"Oh." Her eyes widened. "*Oh*."

I fought the urge to say anything more. Shannon told me to just ask the question and wait for her answer. But this is torture. After what seemed like hours but was probably less than ten seconds, she spoke.

"Can I let you know?" she asked. "I want to check with Granny Vi. Now that I'm living with her, sometimes she makes plans for us without telling me."

"Yeah, sure."

Anjannette approached before I could say anything else. We've been in each other's company a few times through the years so no introductions were necessary. Once the pleasantries were out of the way, she looked at Keera.

"Sorry to interrupt, but it's time for the next routine."

"Hopefully we'll have willing volunteers like last time," she said then turned her attention back to me. "I'll let you know. If not later today, then definitely tomorrow."

That's not the response I'd been hoping for, but it's better than a no. So at least there's hope.

CHAPTER 4

Keera

Anjannette flopped onto the couch and I sat in the chair across from her.

"That was fucking amazing," she said.

"Yeah it was."

I stretched my legs and propped my feet on the small table between us. A few of our students had stayed to help clean up so we were done in no time.

"Definitely better than the one we held after I first opened the studio. We sat here alone most of the day."

"It wasn't that bad, but today was definitely better," I said. "Classes have been pretty full recently, but I'm thinking after this, there's going to be a waitlist. You should be so proud of the community you've built here, Anjannette. It's amazing."

"I couldn't have done it without you."

"It's been my pleasure." I blinked back tears. "After all,

you saved me from having to find another soul-sucking corporate job."

"Speaking of your corporate job." She shifted sideways and rested her elbow against the armrest. "Let's talk about Simon."

"What about him?"

"It was obvious I interrupted something between the two of you earlier. Did you think I wasn't going to ask?"

"I'd kind of hoped you wouldn't."

"Why? What happened?"

"He asked me to go out to dinner," I said. "Just the two of us," I added just in case that wasn't clear.

"I *told* you he's into you. What did you say?"

"After the initial shock wore off, I told him I needed to check with Granny Vi and I'd let him know."

"Why didn't you just say 'yes'?"

"I don't know if I'm going to."

"Why not?"

"Because he's..." I gestured helplessly. "Simon."

"What does that even mean?"

"I've never thought of him that way and don't know if I want to start."

"From what you've always said, he's a great guy."

"He definitely is," I said. "Simon is super smart and really sweet. He's just not my type."

"Isn't that a good thing?"

"What do you mean?"

She dropped her feet to the floor and sat forward.

"You definitely have a type, just like I did. And you've been working with Dr. Green long enough to have established the fact that your type isn't healthy for you." When I didn't deny or acknowledge her words, she continued. "The guys you dated were all tall and good looking, but they were dicks and treated you like shit. Of course, I didn't realize it at the time because the guys I dated treated me just as bad."

"But now you have Leo, and he treats you like a princess," I said, hoping to deflect the conversation from me.

"Exactly! And he's different from anyone else I ever dated."

"You two are truly made for each other."

"And what if I didn't give him a chance because he 'wasn't my type?'"

"Don't act like you met Leo and it was smooth sailing. It took a little nudging to get you to go out with him."

"That's because I was scared to death of dating again," she said. "Plus, I figured there was no way Leo was as perfect as he seemed."

"And yet he is."

As if talking about the man summoned him, Leo Marakis appeared at the threshold.

"Don't you two look comfy?" He walked across the studio and sat next to Anjannette. Wrapping his arm around her waist, he pulled her closer to him and gave her a quick kiss. "How was the open house?"

"It was amazing," Anjannette said. "The studio was full most of the day and everyone seemed to have a great time."

He listened as we filled him in on the details and even asked questions, truly interested. Whenever I mentioned pole to Brian, or any of my former boyfriends, they barely listened.

It's funny, I grew up with parents who adore each other. They're partners in every sense of the word. So were my grandparents. Yet I ended up dating a string of guys who belittled and berated me.

The thing is that none of them did it in an obvious way. It's like that old saying about how if you put a frog in boiling water it'll jump out. But if you place it in and slowly turn up the heat, it'll allow itself to be boiled alive. And that's exactly what happened with every guy I dated. They subtly insulted me and by the time they were obvious about it, I was too beaten down to leave.

"Keera? Are you okay?"

Based on Anjannette's tone, I'm guessing it wasn't the first time she said my name.

"Sorry, I think all my adrenalin from the day is wearing off."

"I hear you. I'm feeling tired too, but mostly I'm hungry," she said. "Leo and I are going to grab a bite to eat. Want to join us?"

"No thanks, I'm going to head home." I stood and smiled down at her. "I have a phone call to make."

She jumped up and pulled me into a tight hug. Loosening her hold just enough to look me in the eye, she glanced over at Leo then met my gaze again.

"Sometimes changing things up pays off."

"Don't start planning the wedding yet. It's just dinner."

"That's a good start."

SIMON

SHANNON AND I GRABBED A BITE TO EAT AFTER THE OPEN house and she shocked the hell out of me by staying in for the second night in a row. Then she surprised me again when she asked if I wanted to play Madden. It's the only video game she really got into and back in the day, she kicked ass. But I figure she won't be as good now since she probably hasn't touched a controller in more than a decade.

We headed down to the basement and I grabbed Madden 07 off the shelf and popped it into the Playstation 2 that's still hooked up to the ancient rear-projection TV. Our parents keep saying they're going to renovate down here, but the closest they've come is replacing the furniture with the old upstairs living room set. Hanging out here is like being in a time warp. Aside from the old TV, our favorite toys through the ages line the built-in shelves throughout the room.

"Do you think they'll ever renovate this space?" Shannon asked.

I'm not surprised our thoughts are on the same wavelength. It happens a lot, even when we're in separate cities.

I sat on the other end of the couch and brought the game to life.

"I'm kind of wondering if they're just gonna sell the house and move."

"Don't even say that."

"Why?"

"This is our childhood home. You wouldn't care if they got rid of it?"

"Not really," I said. "I mean, it'd be weird, but I'd survive."

"I'd hate it."

She shifted and sat cross-legged on the couch. Resting her elbows on her knees, she held the controller in a death grip, and shifted her attention to the TV. I guess she's ready to play.

The memory card is still in the console so I flipped through our saved games and clicked, bringing Madden graphics to life on the screen. Soon the room was filled with the sound of the video game interspersed with controller clicks and smack talk.

Either her muscle memory is exceptional or Shannon has played recently because she's as good as she was as a teen. Insults roll right off her back so I decided to play dirty.

"Would you really hate it if mom and dad sold the house?"

Her slight hesitation gave me the opening I needed to score another touchdown. With the way she's playing, I need to get a good lead early.

"You suck," she said as we lined our teams up again. "But to answer your question, yes it would bother me."

"Why?"

"What do you mean *why*?"

"You technically haven't lived here since high school."

"I know, but I love this house. I can't imagine not coming home for holidays or to visit."

"I can't argue with that." I groaned as Shannon took out my quarterback with a perfect blitz, then added, "In case you're worried, they haven't mentioned selling the house. That was just something I threw out there."

"Good to know."

I haven't played this particular game in a while either so I really had to concentrate to keep my lead. Sports aren't my thing, but they are my dad's. He played Division 1 football, but it was pretty obvious after playing one season of youth football that it just wasn't for me. When I got my first Playstation, there were sports games wrapped up along with my preferred sci-fi titles. Through the years, my dad and I spent hours playing together. He taught me sports lingo and strategy and I showed him the ins and outs of gaming. Perfect quality time for a jock dad and his nerdy son.

"Keera seems nice."

My hands jerked and I messed up the play I was trying to execute. I glanced at Shannon out of the corner of my eye as our players settled at the line of scrimmage. Guess I'm not the only one playing dirty.

"Yeah, she's great."

"She's really pretty too."

"MmmHmm."

"The models I know would love to have her hair. It's so thick," she said. "And her eyes are gorgeous. Would you say they're more ocean or sapphire?"

A mental picture of Keera popped into my mind.

Caribbean blue.

My family took a vacation to Barbados when I was thirteen and I never forgot the color of the ocean there. It's the most beautiful thing I'd ever seen. Until Keera. Her eyes are the same amazing shade.

But I'm not sharing that with Shannon.

"No idea."

"I kind of wish we stayed to see her routine. That would have been fun."

I'm not sure *fun* is the word I'd use.

Watching Keera's lush curves moving to the beat of whatever sexy song was playing would have been more like torture.

"Yes!"

That single word brought my full attention back to the game. Shannon scored another touchdown to tie the score.

"I can't believe you hustled me."

"How did I hustle you?" she asked around a chuckle.

"I assumed you haven't played in years, but that's not the case, is it?"

"I may have played a time or two." She shrugged. "And you know what you get when you assume."

We're coming to the end of the game and I'll never hear the end of it if I let her beat me. I shifted forward, hyper concentrating on the TV screen.

At the end of the fourth quarter, the score was still tied and I had control of the ball. She blitzed me on the first down and I had an incomplete pass on the second. On the third, I found a hole and decided to make a run for it. Shannon wasn't expecting that and it took her a beat to adjust, which gave me the head start I needed.

My guy was on his way to a touchdown when my phone buzzed. Out of the corner of my eye, I saw Keera's name pop up on the screen and the controller bobbled in my hand, making my player fumble the ball.

Shannon's guy grabbed it, but instead of trying to tackle him before he got too far, I put my controller on the couch next to me and picked up my phone.

"Hi. Keera. How's it going?"

"I'm good," she said. "I'm calling about dinner Wednesday."

The tone of her voice wasn't giving me any clues to whether her answer would be positive or negative. My stomach tightened.

"Uh huh."

Stupid response, but I had no idea what else to say.

"I'd love to go out with you."

"Great."

We chatted a few minutes more, mostly about details for Wednesday night before hanging up. I may have just lost a video game to my sister, but I can't complain because I got the girl. Hopefully.

CHAPTER 5

Keera

I FOLDED FORWARD AND SHOOK OUT THE CURLS THEN FLIPPED my hair back and scrunched it into place. After getting each strand situated the way I like, I sprayed the hell out of it. Once I had it thoroughly doused, I stepped back and studied my reflection.

I'm not sure where Simon is taking me, but my black knee-length boho dress should work for pretty much any venue. I bought it on sale over a year ago. How sad is it that it's taken me so long to wear? Especially since I love it so much.

The flowy fabric is comfortable, but the smocked waist nips the material in so it skims my curves without accentuating anything I don't want to draw attention to. And speaking of drawing attention. For the first time in years, I wrestled the girls into a push-up bra so they sit high enough to peek above the V-neck. They look spectacular, if I do say so myself.

Happy with my choice of clothing for the evening, I leaned forward to get a closer look at my makeup. My lipstick isn't bleeding and there's no mascara under my eyes so I called it good. I shut off the light and headed toward my closet to find some appropriate shoes.

Simon is only a few inches taller than me so I don't want to wear heels. I slipped my feet into a pair of tan booties and checked them out in the mirror. They're okay, but not the look I'm going for tonight. I took them off, placed them back on the shelf, and grabbed a pair of black flats. With pointed toes and sleek straps that wrap around my ankles, they're perfect.

I walked over to my jewelry box and pulled out a long silver chain adorned colorful dragonfly pendant. After slipping it over my head, I added a few bracelets and rings. I used to wear my silver stack rings and fire opal all the time, but now they feel foreign on my fingers. Since I can't wear rings at the studio because they'll scratch the poles, I stopped wearing them altogether once I started working there full-time.

Studying myself in the mirror one last time, I felt satisfied with the image reflected back at me. Granny Vi was right. It's been too long since I took the time to make myself look nice. I vowed to do it regularly going forward. Date or no date.

Speaking of Granny Vi. She was sitting in her recliner waiting for me as I entered the living room.

"Well, don't you look nice."

"Thanks."

"Where's he taking you?"

"We're going out to dinner, but I'm not sure where."

"Are you nervous?"

"Why would I be nervous?"

I dropped my big purse on the coffee table and sat on the couch across from her. Retrieving my ID, cash, lip balm, and keys from the bag, I placed them into my small clutch and added my phone.

When she didn't answer, I looked over at her.

"It's been a while since you went on a date." She smirked. "And the last time you were on a date with a normal guy is never."

"Gee, thanks."

"I'm serious. None of those guys you dated before were worth anything."

"You don't even know Simon. How do you know what he's worth?"

"Because the two of you have been friends for years," she said. "And you do pick good friends. It's the lovers you have trouble with."

"Eewww, Granny Vi, don't say that."

"Lovers," she said again, this time dragging the words out using a low, sexy voice.

The doorbell rang and I breathed a sigh of relief that our conversation couldn't continue.

"Saved by the bell," I muttered.

I did a double take as I opened the door. The man standing across the threshold is *not* who I was expecting. Instead of my nerdy former co-worker, in front of me is Simon 2.0.

His ginger hair normally runs amuck, but he obviously got a good cut and tonight some kind of product has it tamed into neat, slicked-back waves. As if that weren't enough, his clothes are different too. Instead of baggy cargo pants and a graphic T-shirt or polo, he has on khakis that look custom fit and one of those fancy button-down shirts made to be worn untucked. The navy and gray checked pattern really brings out his eyes. Or maybe I'm just noticing them more because he's not wearing glasses.

"Don't just stand there gawking, let the man in," Granny Vi said.

"Sorry," I said and stood back, allowing Simon to enter. "You just look so different," I said, then quickly added, "Without your glasses."

He flashed an adorably shy smile and I placed my hand on my stomach to calm the little flutter that came out of nowhere.

"I got contacts a while ago and figured I might as well take them out for a spin." Holding up a bouquet I hadn't noticed in his left hand, he said, "These are for you."

I took the flowers from him and smiled. The bright, bold fall colors are interspersed with black pansies and lilies. Simon really knows me. Even though I've toned it down since my teen years, I'm a goth girl at heart.

"Thank you. I love them."

Before going to put them in water, I introduced Simon to Granny Vi.

"It's nice to meet you, Mrs. Jordan. I've heard a lot about you," he said.

"Same," she said. "The flowers are a nice touch."

I debated leaving them alone because I have no idea what Granny Vi will say, but the flowers need water. Besides, if this goes beyond one date, he might as well get used to her lack of filter.

Their voices carried into the kitchen but I couldn't hear what they were saying. I retrieved a vase from the cabinet and filled it with water. After snipping the bottom of the stems, I dropped each flower in and shifted them around until I was happy with the arrangement.

I walked back into the living room, happy to hear

Granny Vi and Simon discussing computers instead of something more intimate. After placing the vase in the middle of the coffee table, I picked up my clutch.

"Ready to go?"

"Sure." Turning his attention back to Granny Vi, he said, "It was nice meeting you."

"It was a pleasure. Where are you kids heading?"

"The AV."

"Nice," Granny Vi said.

Simon followed me to the door then reached behind me to open it. I was about to step outside when I realized I forgot my sweater.

I ran back to my room and grabbed it off the bed. Granny Vi called me over to her when I returned to the living room. Gesturing for me to lean down, she whispered in my ear.

"He's looking like a winner." She looked over toward the door and shifted her eyes down, giving Simon a pants check, then smirked as she met my gaze. "In more ways than one."

I preceded Simon out the door, thanking every holy entity known to man she hadn't said that loud enough for him to hear.

SIMON

"It was nice meeting your grandmother after hearing about her for so long."

"I'm just happy she didn't say anything inappropriate." Her eyes widened. "She didn't, did she? When I was in the kitchen?"

"No, she asked me about computers."

"What could she possibly want to know about computers?"

"Her laptop is running slow and her casino games keep freezing."

"So what did you tell her?"

"I said to clear her cache and cookies, which she said she knows how to do. If that doesn't work, I told her I'll take a look at it."

"That was so nice of you."

"Anything for a friend. Or her grandmother."

I couldn't put a name to the look that crossed her face at my words, but the waitress approached with our meals and it was replaced with a smile before I had a chance to really study it.

"This all looks amazing," Keera said.

We'd ordered individual salads, but for the main course, decided to split a few small plates. We took a sampling and shared our thoughts on each one. My favorite is the porcini cavatappi and Keera's is the grilled octopus. But to be honest, it's all delicious.

"I knew you had a sister, but I don't think you ever told me you guys are twins. Did you?"

I shrugged as I finished chewing a bite of crostini slathered with whipped honey goat cheese.

"Probably not. When we were younger, I'd mention it because we were in the same grade, but now it seems kind of weird to say 'my twin' unless it comes up somehow. And since we're fraternal, I don't have any funny stories about how we switched places and got away with it or people mistook us for each other." I chuckled. "We don't even look like we're related, much less twins."

"You really don't resemble each other at all. How is that possible?"

"I look like my mom and she looks like my dad."

Keera popped a calamari into her mouth and nodded as she chewed.

"Is she still in town?"

"No, she was just visiting for the weekend."

"She lives in Manhattan, right?" Since my mouth was full, I just nodded. "Does she come home often?"

I really don't want to spend dinner talking about Shannon, so I searched my brain for a new topic. I've never dated a friend before, so coming up with something isn't easy. Normally, first date conversation is spent getting to know basic facts about the person. I already know those details about Keera.

When nothing came to mind, I decided to just go with the flow. After all, we *are* friends. We shouldn't act differently just because this is a date. Spending time with Keera has always been easy and I don't want that to change. So I decided to treat this like the myriad conversations we've had through the years.

"She works with a few fashion photographers, so her schedule gets a little crazy at certain times of the year, but she manages to come home often enough."

"So your sister works with fancy photographers, your mom makes vaccines, and your dad is a reporter for ESPN. That's some pretty cool shit."

I shrugged.

"I guess so."

"And I've known you for how long and never met them?"

"They don't frequent Party on the Patio like your family does."

We used to go to the free weekly concerts at the

Mohegan Sun Casino in the summer with a gang from work. Keera's parents were often there so I've met them a few times.

"That's because your family is off doing exotic things," she said. "Like this extended road trip your parents are on now. That's so cool."

"It's something my dad has always wanted to do."

"Are they enjoying themselves?"

"So far, which I'll admit is surprising. I thought my mom would be begging to come home after a month, but it's been almost three and she still seems happy."

"When will they be back?"

"They're coming home for a month over Thanksgiving and Christmas then heading out again for another six months. So they'll be gone for twelve months total."

"And you're staying at their house?"

"Yeah, it got me out of that crappy studio for now. I'll start looking for a place after the new year," I said. "What about you?"

"What about me?"

"You're living with Granny Vi?"

"For now. After my grandfather died, she didn't like living alone. Not that she'd admit that to anyone, but it was pretty obvious she wasn't happy." She took a sip of water. "So when I left Brian, I asked if I could stay with her until I found a place."

"And it's working out okay?"

"It is. Even though she can drive me crazy, she's literally my favorite person in the world. And I like being there just in case she needs me, you know? I mean, for the most part, she's in good health, but like she always likes to tell me, she's not getting any younger."

The waitress came over to clear the now-empty dishes.

"Are you interested in dessert?" she asked.

"Oh um..."

Keera looked at me, seeming unsure. I know she has a huge sweet tooth, so that surprised the hell out of me. I figured she'd already know what she wants, considering she's been eyeing the desserts being carried through the restaurant. I'm feeling full after our meal, but not so stuffed that dessert is out of the question.

"What do you have?" I asked.

She recited a list, but two caught my attention." I looked at Keera. "I can't decide between the cannoli and limoncello cake. Want to share?"

"Oh..." She licked her lips then shook her head. "I shouldn't."

Through the years, I've heard Keera complain about her weight. I've also watched her try every fad diet and I just don't get it. The woman has curves in all the right places and I have no idea why she'd want to change that.

"That doesn't mean you *can't*."

Keera blinked and chuckled at my raised brow, then turned her attention to the waitress.

"We'll share the cannoli and limoncello cake."

CHAPTER 6

Keera

Simon pulled into the driveway and I'll admit, I'm sad for the night to end. He'd taken back roads to my house instead of the interstate, so he must feel the same way.

After shifting the car into park, he turned to face me.

"Thanks for coming out with me tonight, Keera. I had a great time."

His eyebrows lifted slightly, as if he'd asked a question.

"I had a great time, too."

And I'm not just saying that. I'll admit I was worried tonight would be weird, but it definitely wasn't. Even though there was a date vibe, I felt just as comfortable as every other time we've gone out. There were no awkward pauses in conversation and I seriously wanted to jump across the table and kiss him when the waitress asked about dessert. After so many years worrying about Brian's reaction to every bite I put into my mouth, it was nice to just enjoy a meal without judgement.

"Would you uh–" He cleared his throat and shifted his eyes to look just above my head. Nodding, he looked at me again and continued. "Would you want to go out again Friday night?"

"I can't. I'm at the studio until ten."

"Oh. Okay."

I hated the disappointment that clouded his eyes.

"But I'm free Saturday if you are."

Simon's eyes widened and a slow smile spread across his face.

"I'm definitely free."

The flashing porch light caught the corner of my eye just as I was about to speak.

"Granny Vi." I nudged my head, directing his attention to the light show my grandmother was putting on. "I've heard stories about how she used to do that to my parents when they were dating. I always thought it was funny, but now I'm not so sure."

"I better let you get inside before she breaks the light fixture," he said with a chuckle.

Granny Vi must have been watching because as soon as Simon got out of the car, the light stopped flashing. He came around to my side and opened the door then held his hand out. I'm an independent woman and as such always said I didn't *need* the guys I dated to do things like that for me. But tonight, I haven't opened a door and I have to say, it's kind of nice.

I took hold of his hand and stepped out of the car and he closed the door behind me. Still holding hands, we walked toward the porch and climbed the four steps that led us to the front door. He turned to face me and took my other hand.

"Are you at the studio Saturday?"

I nodded.

"Until two."

"I'll pick you up at six?"

"Perfect."

"Great." He squeezed my hands then slowly released them. "I guess I'll see you then."

I nodded and reached up to tuck my hair behind my ear. We stood there for a few seconds more, just staring into each other's eyes.

I've gone out with guys since Brian and I split, but they were pretty much just planned hookups, sometimes with a meal beforehand. But it's been a long time since I had a real first date, complete with a pre-kiss moment like Simon and I are having now.

My heart pounded as he took a step closer and placed his hands on my waist. I'd be lying if I didn't admit that it's kind of strange. I mean, this is *Simon*. In all the years we've known each other, I've *never* thought about kissing him.

Yet here I am unable to think of anything else.

I took a deep breath in through my nose and let it out the same way as Simon's hand slowly skimmed up my side and settled onto the side of my neck. He stroked the underside of my jaw with his thumb, seeming to give me time to back away. Not only did I not back away, I leaned into his touch and looked down at his mouth.

He whispered my name and I shifted my eyes up to look into his. My heart raced as he moved his head forward a fraction, then stopped and searched my gaze, giving me one last chance to retreat. When I didn't, he tunneled his fingers through my hair and touched his mouth to mine.

The kiss wasn't much more than a soft brushing of lips, but it made my heart pound double-time. I let out a shuddering sigh as Simon slid his hand to cup the back of my head then moaned against his mouth as he pressed it fully against mine.

Wanting to get closer, I wrapped my arms around his neck. He moved his hand to the small of my back and pulled me even closer as his mouth opened, deepening the kiss, and adding a soft suction that made my lady parts tingle. That feeling intensified when he touched his tongue to mine, taking the kiss to a whole other level.

It went on and on and I got lost in the sensation, forgetting the fact that I'm standing on my front porch making out with Simon Parker. Part of my brain kept insisting this should be weird, but it doesn't feel weird. It feels very right.

I felt like I was floating, then realized Simon was actually walking me back toward the house. Soon I found myself sandwiched between cold brick and warm man, his hand still cradling my head, protecting it from the hard surface.

He pulled his mouth from mine for a split second and tilted his head to the other side to go at the kiss from a different angle. Different, but just as good. I dug my fingers into his scalp as our tongues tangled together, the kiss going on and on, building in intensity.

I have no idea how long we were at it, but in my mind, it wasn't long enough.

Releasing the back of my head, Simon's hand skimmed against my neck, across my shoulder, and stopped at the side of my breast. My heart pounded even harder in anticipation, but instead of cupping me like I thought...*hoped*...he would, he slid it lower to rest against my waist and slowly ended the kiss.

"I uh–" He cleared his throat. "I should let you get inside before Granny Vi comes out looking for you."

It took a second for my befuddled brain to make sense of his words, but then I nodded.

"Thanks again for a great night."

"I'll see you Saturday," he said before slowly backing away.

"See you Saturday."

He opened the door and I stepped inside, turning to watch as he walked down the steps and made his way to his car. He opened the driver's side door and with a wave, sat behind the wheel and started the engine. I waited until he backed out of the driveway and pulled down the street before closing the door behind me. Resting my back against it, I placed my fingers on my tingling lips.

"How was your date?" Granny Vi asked from her recliner.

She's not going to let me sneak off to my room without giving some details. As I walked toward the couch, I tried to figure out what to tell her, but there were only four words running through my head.

Simon Parker. Holy hell.

SIMON

I CIRCLED THE BLOCK TWICE THEN FOUND AN EMPTY SPOT AND backed in. As I stepped out of the car, I looked up at the apartment building and remembered I don't live here anymore. I shook my head then slipped back behind the wheel. Thankfully I didn't head inside. That would have been embarrassing.

I'd just pulled back onto the road when my phone rang. I accepted the call and my sister's voice filled the car.

"It must have been a hell of a date if you forgot where you live."

"What are you talking about?"

"I just watched you drive to your old apartment building."

"What?" I looked around at the empty road. "You're *tracking* me?"

"Don't sound so surprised. You know we share our locations with each other and mom and dad."

"Yeah, but I never stalk you."

I swear I heard her eyes roll through the phone.

"I was just curious about how your date went and checked to see if you were home so I could call and ask." She chuckled. "And again, I'm guessing it went well since you forgot where you live."

The date was amazing, and that kiss was insane. Better than I ever imagined, and trust me when I say, I've imagined. But I'm not sharing those details with my sister.

"We're going out again Saturday night, so it must have gone well."

"Simon."

She drew out my name like she does either when she's excited about something or mad at me. I'm assuming it's the former right now.

"So where are you taking her?" she asked.

"I'm not sure."

"What do you mean *you're not sure?*"

"Shan, I just dropped her off. Give me a minute."

"I can *give* you some suggestions."

My first instinct is to tell her 'no,' but didn't just in case I don't think of anything on my own.

"Let me see what I come up with and I'll let you know if I need help."

I turned into my parents' driveway and opened the garage door then pulled inside.

"Home again, home again," Shannon said.

"I'm shutting off my location."

Her laugh echoed through the garage as I stepped out of the car.

"Mom would freak out."

I pressed the button to close the garage door and walked into the kitchen. I was about to tell Shannon that our mom is too busy enjoying her trip to worry about checking on me when I realized that if my sister is paying attention to what I'm doing, she must not be out.

"How come you're home stalking me instead of painting the town with the beautiful people?"

"I went out to dinner with Juliet and Paisley, but came home right after."

"Hell must be freezing over."

"No, I just wasn't feeling it."

Right after graduating from esthetics school, Shannon passed her licensing test and was offered a paid internship at L'Oréal in Manhattan. She'd always wanted to move to the big city so given the chance, she took it and never looked back.

She loves her career and especially loves living in the city. Between business events and going out with her friends, she always has something to do. I could count on one hand the number of nights she's stayed in over the past decade. It's even more interesting considering she was here last weekend and didn't go out either.

"Everything okay?"

I walked up the stairs and headed toward my bedroom,

eager to take out my contact lenses. I've only had them in for six hours but they're driving me crazy.

"Hmm, yeah. For the most part," she said. "But this call isn't to talk about me. It's to figure out how my big brother is going to sweep the girl of his dreams off her feet."

I stepped into my bathroom, placed my phone on the counter, and put Shannon on speaker.

"However I do it, I'm hoping I won't need to wear these contact lenses all the time."

"You have nice eyes, but they're usually hidden behind your glasses. Show them off once in a while."

Keera did seem to focus on my eyes a lot, so Shannon might be on to something. She was definitely right about my hair and clothes. The cut she gave me is pretty easy to tame with the product she showed me how to use. And the fitted khakis and button-down shirt make me look more like a grownup than a college student.

"Maybe I just need to wear them more to get used to them."

I pinched the right lens between my thumb and forefinger and placed it in its case, then did the same with the left. Rubbing my eyes offered some relief and splashing them with cold water soothed the itchy picky feeling they've had the past few hours.

"Maybe," she said, seeming distracted all of a sudden. "I have another call coming in that I have to take. Let me know what you decide to do Saturday."

"Okay. Talk to you later."

Something is definitely going on with Shannon these days. I mentally shrugged and unbuttoned my shirt as I walked into my bedroom. I don't usually butt into her business like she does mine. If it's something important, she'll eventually share.

I undressed, tossing my clothes onto the chair in the corner, then slipped under the covers. Normally I play video games or read before bed, but tonight I'm just going to lie here, think about the past few hours, and figure out where to take Keera Saturday night.

CHAPTER 7

Keera

"It was really nice," I said. "I mean, I thought it would be weird because we've been friends for so long, but it wasn't."

I managed to avoid questions before and during class, but now that it's over, a few of the ladies stayed behind just to hear the details of my date with Simon. Anjannette even took my class instead of heading home after hers like she normally does on Thursday nights.

"But did it feel like a date or just a night out with a friend?" Sophie asked.

"Somehow it felt like both." Three sets of eyes stared at me, demanding details. "Simon and I have been friends for years so we didn't have to do the whole getting-to-know-you dance. The conversation was the same as the countless ones we've had before..." I trailed off and tried to figure out a way to describe the night. "There was definitely a spark between us which was new, but the comfortable, relaxed feeling was there too."

"Please tell me it ended with a kiss worthy of one of my novels," Eve said.

I looked over at her and burst into laughter.

"What?" she asked. "Indulge me, please. It's been *way* too long since I had a date. Or a kiss for that matter."

"Yes there was a kiss." Leaning forward, I rested my elbows against my knees. "And *yes*, it was worthy of one of your romance novels."

"Please tell me more, I could use some inspiration. I've barely written a word since the divorce and that was almost three years ago. Thankfully I had some books stockpiled so there hasn't been a huge gap in my release schedule."

Yes, when Eve says one of her romance novels, she literally means one of *her* novels. Both she and Sophie are bestselling authors. They're also to blame for my addiction to romance books. I was always a horror/thriller girl, but when Sophie joined the studio, I decided to check out one of her books and have been hooked since.

"He walked me to the door and at first it seemed like he was going to leave without a kiss, but then he made his move. I'll admit that when his lips first touched mine, I kept thinking it should be weird because it was Simon. But it wasn't. And when he deepened the kiss, all thoughts left my brain and I could only focus on him and the moment. It was pretty amazing. I mean, who knew Simon Parker could kiss like that?"

As if they'd rehearsed it, the three women let out a collective *awwww*.

"Are you going out with him again?" Anjannette asked.

I nodded.

"Saturday night."

"So you like him?" Sophie asked. "I mean *like him*, like him."

"Are we in middle school?"

"Just answer the question," Eve said, sounding more like a judge than a writer.

I didn't have to think about my answer because I've been pondering that same question since yesterday.

"I do," I said. "Honestly, if I didn't feel something, I wouldn't have agreed to a second date. Simon is a good guy and I wouldn't want to lead him on."

"You worked with him all those years and there was never anything between you?" Sophie asked.

"I was dating Jason when Simon first started working at Wilder, then Brian. And at one point, Simon had a girlfriend and they lived together for a while. I just never looked at him as anything more than a friend."

"But now..." Anjannette said and made a kissy-face.

"He also did something that I never thought I'd like, but I did."

"Do tell," Sophie said. "I'll take notes for my current work in progress."

"Get your mind out of the gutter," I said. "He held doors open for me, opened the car door, held out his hand to help me out of the car. Gentlemanly stuff like that. Hell, he even walked me to the door at the end of the night. None of the guys I dated ever did that. Granny Vi and my mom commented on it more than once, especially with Brian, but I told them that kind of thing was old-fashioned and outdated."

"But it's not," Anjannette said. "I'm with you, none of my exes did it, or if they did, it was short-lived. But Leo does that stuff all the time. I'm the same as you, I never thought I'd like it, but I do. It's really sweet."

"Good for you two ladies finding the good guys. It's just like our books," Eve said.

"And you both deserve the best."

"Let's not get ahead of ourselves here. Simon and I have had one date. So what you said really only applies to Anjannette and Leo."

"Oh please," Anjannette said. "For years I said that Simon had the hots for you. Now that you're giving him a chance, the only way it's not going to turn into something more is if you don't want it to."

I'd be lying if I said her words didn't freak me out a little. Or a lot. Simon is the nicest guy I've ever dated and I don't want to hurt him. What if I'm just talking myself into feeling something? What if this moves forward and I find I'm *not* not into him? Or even worse, what if I don't know how to function in a *normal* relationship?

"Stop it!" Anjannette's words stopped my spiraling thoughts. Once she had my attention, she continued. "Stop thinking yourself out of a relationship with Simon before it has a chance to get started."

"Says the woman who's in the perfect relationship," I said then hoped my tone was more snarky than sarcastic.

"And you were there every step of the way to make sure I didn't go off the rails when Leo and I first got together. Hell, if it wasn't for you, I probably wouldn't have even given him a chance. So now it's your turn to listen. You're amazing and you deserve to be happy. Simon is wonderful and sweet and kind, and given the chance, he'll treat you like the queen you are."

Anjannette stood and mimicked a mic drop, then walked over to the couch and grabbed her duffle bag and purse. "And now I'm going home to *my* perfect man. See you tomorrow ladies."

I watched her leave then looked at Sophie and Eve, my brows raised.

"She's not wrong you know," Sophie said.

"She definitely isn't," Eve agreed.

If my girls all believe it, it must be true. They wouldn't steer me wrong.

Now I just have to convince myself.

Simon

"Do you guys need anything else while I'm in here?" I yelled.

"Napkins," Andrew said.

Archer didn't answer so I figured he's good. After grabbing three bottles of Susquehanna Brewing Pumpkin Ale and a stack of napkins, I made my way back into the living room. My friends were sprawled on the couch, each holding a heaping plate of Chinese food.

I placed the beer on the coffee table and filled my own plate before settling on the recliner.

"You ready?"

"As I'll ever be," Archer said.

Normally we play video games on Thursday nights, but I'm not feeling that so I suggested watching *Obi-Wan Kenobi* instead. Archer's not thrilled with the change, but since Andrew is okay with it, majority rules. I reached for the remote and turned on the TV.

"Wait," Andrew said. "Aren't you going to tell us about your date?"

"Uh, it seemed to go well." I shrugged. "We're going out again Saturday, so…"

"Where'd you take her?"

This again from Andrew. When it comes to dating, he's kind of stuck, so he's always interested in what other people are doing. Archer could care less, both about having a love life or hearing about anyone else's.

"The AV."

"Nice. That's on my list of places to go," Andrew said. "It's definitely a good first date location."

"I'm glad you approve."

He totally missed my sarcasm.

"I should ask someone out on a date, you know, get back out there. There's a new physical therapist at work. Maybe I'll ask her out."

"In my opinion, work isn't the best place to meet women. What if she says no? Or she says yes then it doesn't work out?" I pointed out. "That's why I never asked Keera out before now."

"Yeah, but where else am I supposed to meet someone?" he asked. "Stacy and I met in college. Work is the adult equivalent to meeting in school, isn't it?"

"Like I said, it's just my opinion."

Andrew and Stacy broke up right after he graduated from medical school. It's been almost ten years but he talks about her like they broke up a month ago. Then again, the dates he's had since haven't gone anywhere, so I guess it's the only big relationship he has to reference.

"Does Keera have any friends you can set me up with?"

"Even if she does, I'm not sure it's a good idea right now."

"Why not?"

"For one thing, Keera and I literally had one date. I have no idea what's going to happen with us."

"Maybe after you're dating a while."

My mom always says Andrew is a great catch, so I don't know why he has such a difficult time with women. He's not socially awkward like Archer and at 6'4", he's not height challenged like me. Add in the fact that he's one of the top orthopedic surgeons in the area, he should be a magnet, but somehow he always either ends up with someone who just wants him because he's a doctor or he gets friend-zoned.

When I was with Zoe, we set him up with one of her friends. Unfortunately that fizzled out after a few dates. I'm not really up for repeating the experience, but he sounded so hopeful, I couldn't do anything but agree.

"If that's settled, can we start watching the show, please?" Archer leaned forward and added a couple dumplings to his plate. "It's bad enough we're off our usual Thursday night schedule, do we need to sit here discussing women all night?"

"Sure."

I picked up the remote again and brought up the app menu, stifling my smile. Shannon always calls my friends and me *The Big Bang* crew and if that's the case, Archer is our Sheldon. The man schedules everything and deviations from said schedule are not welcome.

Andrew and I push him out of his comfort zone sometimes. He grumbles about it, but hey, the three of us have been friends since grade school and he still hangs around with us so he must not totally hate it.

Since we're not gaming, he's really not enjoying himself tonight, but surprisingly, hasn't complained too much. He didn't even comment when I ordered kung pao shrimp instead of my usual sweet and sour chicken.

After pressing play on *Obi-Wan Kenobi*, I sat back to watch and dug into my Chinese food, savoring the different flavors. Sometimes it's nice to do something different or think outside the box. After all, doing the same thing and expecting a different result is the definition of insanity.

I've been stuck in a rut for a while now. My days have become as predictable as Archer's. But ever since I decided to ask Keera out, it's like something shifted in me. I don't want to live a *Groundhog Day* existence, repeating the same day over and over anymore. It's time to do different things, be spontaneous, and enjoy life.

And hopefully Keera will be part of that.

CHAPTER 8

Keera

"ARE YOU SURE I'M DRESSED OKAY?"

"You look perfect," Simon said. "I like the pole studio's slogan."

I looked down at my sweatshirt with *No ifs...just good butts* printed across the chest, then smiled.

"Yeah, we get a lot of compliments on it."

He'd told me to dress comfortably for our date so I wore leggings and a Peaches & Pole hoodie. He's wearing jeans and a Star Wars tee, but I still feel like I should have on something nicer. We had a casual dinner at Joyce's Café and now we're back in the car heading who knows where.

When I asked where we're going, he told me it's a surprise, so I'm trying to accept that answer and not bug him about it. I crossed my legs and settled into the seat as we merged onto the Scranton-Carbondale Highway.

"So how were your classes today?" he asked.

"Good. Both were totally full which is great for the

studio, but it made for a busy day. Thankfully I didn't plan anything too difficult because I had to demonstrate the moves multiple times for the two groups in each class."

"It seems like things are really doing well there. The open house was packed."

"Yeah, the place was full the entire time. And the first beginner series we planned was

totally booked that day so we planned another and that's full now too."

"As much as I miss working with you, I'm so happy you're doing what you love."

"Getting laid off was definitely a blessing in disguise." I looked over at him. "Even

though I was freaking out at the time."

"They were crazy to let you go."

He flicked on his blinker and moved into the middle lane to turn left. I looked up and spotted the Circle Drive-In sign.

"We're going to the drive in?" I asked, bouncing in my seat.

"We are."

As he made the turn, I took a second to read the sign.

"The *Rocky Horror Picture Show*?" He nodded. "That's one of my favorites."

He looked over at me and smiled, then pulled up to the ticket booth to pay before making our way to the large parking lot. After he backed into a spot and turned off the engine, we stepped out of the car.

"I haven't been here in years," I said.

"Me neither, but when I saw what was playing, I thought it would make a great second date. Thankfully the weather cooperated."

"It's a perfect night for this."

I followed as he walked around to the back of his Subaru Outback and opened the hatch. A foam mattress covered the back and there were multiple blankets and pillows on top.

"I figured we'd be more comfortable back here."

"This is exactly what my family used to do when I was a kid in our station wagon. Of course, my brother and I had to wear pajamas, so now I feel a little *overdressed*."

"Shannon and I used to wear our pajamas too."

He crawled into the car, grabbed a blanket, and spread it over the foam then placed two big pillows against the back seat. They were the kind with arms that you can recline against.

"My brother and I had pillows like that when we were younger," I said. "They're probably still somewhere at my mom's house."

"These are mine and Shannon's from when we were kids. They're really comfortable," he said. "Do you want popcorn?"

I scrunched my nose.

"I'm kind of full from that ginormous burger I had at Joyce's, but coming to the drive-in and not getting popcorn seems like a crime."

"I totally agree." He held out his hand. "Come on, let's go get some."

I'VE SEEN THE *ROCKY HORROR PICTURE SHOW* MULTIPLE TIMES in a variety of theatres, but never at the drive-in. It was so much fun. People got out of their cars to sing and dance and a few even ran through the aisles of cars throwing various props. By the time the movie was over, the pavement of the parking lot was littered with rice, confetti, and toilet paper.

Simon and I joined in to dance the Time Warp. That's something none of my past boyfriends would have ever done. Then again, none of them would come to see the movie.

We were quiet on the ride back to Granny Vi's. Our joined hands rested on the console and Simon's thumb stroked the back of mine in a slow, steady rhythm.

For years I just thought of Simon as a friend, but that's definitely not the case anymore, which still blows my mind when I focus on it. Yes, we've only had two dates, but I can definitely see this developing into something more. He's so thoughtful and sweet, and I feel good when I'm with him.

As for physical attraction, we definitely have chemistry. Instead of a hot burst like I've felt with guys before, it's more of a warm, comfortable burn. That might be a bad explanation, but all I know is that I'd like to explore it at some point.

The question is *when*?

SIMON

I PULLED INTO THE DRIVEWAY, PUT THE CAR INTO PARK, AND killed the engine. Letting go of Keera's hand, I shifted and rested my forearm against the back of her seat.

"I could hear your mind spinning all the way here. What's up?"

"Tonight was really fun," she said. "Thank you."

"It was and you're welcome. But you're not getting off that easy." I raised my right brow. "What were you thinking about?"

She blinked at me then shook her head.

"It was nothing. Just silly thoughts." I looked at her, letting the silence grow until she felt the need to speak. "This is our second date and when I really think about it, it's just–" She flipped her hand back and forth a couple times before completing the thought. "–it's still strange."

"Why?"

"Because you're *Simon*," she said with a nervous chuckle. "In all the years we've known each other, I never thought about us dating."

"Oh." I thought about that for a second, then asked. "And now?"

The corner of her mouth kicked up into an adorable smile.

"I can't keep the thought out of my mind."

"That's good."

I tucked her hair behind her ear, cupped her cheek, and leaned in. There was no hesitancy like the other night. She met me halfway, and as soon as our mouths touched, the heat our kiss generated nearly melted me in my seat. Our tongues teased and tangled, and I groaned when she threaded her fingers through my hair and held on.

Only one word ran through my mind. *More.*

Wrapping my arms around her waist, I pulled her across the console until her upper body pressed against mine. Her full breasts flattened against my chest and I tightened my hold, pulling her closer still. Our hearts pounded in a matching rhythm as the kiss went on and on.

She released my hair and wrapped her arms around my neck, pulling me closer as our mouths continued to feast. Still holding her tight, I leaned back in my seat, practically pulling her onto my lap. I moved my hands over her lush body, savoring every single dip and curve. Not able to resist any longer, I moved my hand up to cup her breast, but before I reached the promised land, heard a loud honk and jumped back, banging my head off the window.

I let out an awkward chuckle and rested my forehead against hers.

"Sorry about that. I bumped the horn with my elbow."

Keera slid back into her seat and I immediately missed her warmth.

"Is your head okay?" she asked.

"Yeah. It'll be fine."

"I should probably get inside anyway." She gestured toward the house. "We don't want Granny Vi putting on a light show again."

"We definitely don't want that."

After giving her a quick kiss, I stepped out of the car, then jogged around to the passenger side and opened her door. She placed her hand in mine and stood. We walked hand in hand across the sidewalk and up the steps to the front porch.

"Thanks for tonight," she said.

"It was my pleasure. Maybe we can do it again sometime?"

"I'd like that."

"Are you free during the week?"

She scrunched her nose in that adorable way she has.

"Not really. Anjannette and I are still putting the finishing touches on the beginners' series so we're staying late to work on that all week. But Saturday should be good."

"Saturday it is. And if you're not too tired during the week when you get home, give me a call."

"I will."

I leaned down and gave her a quick kiss then opened the screen door and stepped back as she unlocked the door.

"Great. I'll talk to you during the week and we'll make plans."

She opened the door and stepped inside then watched until I got back behind the wheel. I waved as I pulled out of the driveway then turned onto the street.

I'll admit I'm bummed things ended the way they did. I finally got my hands on her and ruined the moment by bumping the horn. Talk about a bonehead move.

But I suppose it's for the best. Because something tells me that once I really get to touch and explore her amazing body, I'm not going to want to stop.

CHAPTER 9

Keera

I PULLED UP IN FRONT OF THE HOUSE, SURPRISED TO SEE MY mom's car in the driveway. Not that she doesn't stop in often, but she's not usually here this late.

Grabbing my duffle bag, I got out of the car and went inside.

"You're home late," my mom said.

"Yeah, we're working on the beginners' series," I said. "I think we're finally done."

"Did you eat?" Granny Vi asked. "There's pizza."

"Thanks, but Leo brought us takeout," I said. "I'll be right back. I want to throw this into the wash."

I walked through the kitchen and into the laundry room. After opening the washing machine lid, I unzipped the duffle and pulled out an assortment of pole shorts and tops and tossed them in. I added a pod, closed the lid, and headed back out to the living room.

My mom and Granny Vi stopped talking as I approached and watched me sit on the couch.

"What's wrong?"

"Nothing," my mom said. "But Granny Vi mentioned that you might have a new beau."

Now I know why my mom's still here. I glared at my grandmother.

"Granny Vi talks too much."

"I didn't know it was supposed to be a secret." she said.

"It's not, but I didn't think it was newsworthy either."

"I wouldn't say it's *newsworthy*, but it is interesting," my mother said. "Simon is your friend that dad and I met at Party on the Patio, right? The one with the reddish hair?"

"Yep."

"So how did the two of you end up together?"

I shifted to sit back against the armrest and crossed my legs.

"He came to the open house at the studio and asked me out."

"Well, I'm glad you agreed to go out with him."

"Why?"

"He's not your usual type, which is a good thing."

Any response I make to that would be snarky, so I didn't comment. Not deterred by

my silence, she continued.

"You should bring him to your dad's show."

My dad has been in a band since the 80's. Despite being named Afternoon Delight, they're actually pretty good and have superfans who go to see them whenever they play.

"Isn't that Thanksgiving weekend?"She nodded. "Mom, that's almost a month away.

Simon and I just had our second date, I can't ask him to do something that far off."

"Why not?"

"I just can't. Not right now anyway," I said. "Maybe closer to the date if we're still hanging out."

"The terms you kids have. Hanging out sounds like you're loitering on the corner," Granny Vi said. "And worse is *talking*. Cora's granddaughter insisted she was just *talking* to a boy and ended up pregnant." She crossed her arms over her chest. "Hmmph, seems like they were doing more than talking."

"We're just *dating*."

I looked at Granny Vi when I said that last word and gave her an is-that-better look? She nodded in response.

"Well, whatever you're doing, I'm glad. From what I remember, he seemed really sweet," my mom said.

"Yeah, he is."

"Don't sound so happy about it."

I shrugged. My mom moved over and held her arms out. Taking her invitation, I shifted into her embrace and rested my head against her shoulder.

"What's wrong, honey?"

I let out a long sigh.

"Simon *is* really sweet. What if I screw this up and he ends up hating me?"

"Why would that happen?"

I sat up to look her in the eye.

"You know my history with men."

"I do."

"So it should be obvious."

"But it's not."

"I end up jumping in, getting obsessed, and messing things up."

My mom and Granny Vi shared a look, then turned their attention back to me.

"What you did is hook up with morons then stay with them because you thought they could be fixed." Granny Vi pointed her index finger at me. "Newsflash, they can *never* be fixed, especially if they don't want to be."

"She's right," my mom said.

"Damn right I am."

My mom gave me a hug, then pulled back.

"Just be yourself and don't overthink things."

I think I can handle the first thing, but can't promise I'll be able to pull off the second.

Simon

I watched Leo Marakis toss his ball down the lane and lean from side to side, as if he could direct it with his body. He knocked down the remaining four pins for a spare, keeping him in the lead. But it's a pretty tight game so it wouldn't take much to change the rankings.

He came and sat beside me as Keera stepped up to the line.

"I was worried about that one. Anjannette is right behind me and we have a little side bet going on this game," he said, then smirked. "Although honestly, even if I lose, I'll still win."

He didn't offer any details and I didn't ask. Something tells me I don't want to know.

When Keera asked if I wanted to go bowling with Anjannette and Leo, I'll admit I wasn't sure how it would go. But so far, it's been fun.

Leo is more down to Earth than I expected him to be. I know I shouldn't stereotype, but the professional athletes I've met weren't very personable. But Leo is great.

"You're pretty good. Do you bowl often?" he asked.

"Not anymore. When I was a kid, my family used to bowl a lot, plus this was a hot spot for birthday parties. How about you? I mean, you're the one in the lead."

"I'm working on muscle memory and luck here. Like yours, my family used to bowl a lot. There was a place within walking distance of our house and it was a fun and affordable night out for a family of eight."

"Eight?"

He nodded.

"Yep, I have five siblings. Two brothers and three sisters," he said. "And we're all super competitive, so as we got older, things got a little crazy."

"Pay attention boys," Anjannette yelled so we could hear her over the music. "It's your turn, Simon."

"Duty calls," I said and walked up to grab my ball.

"Good luck."

That from Keera who stood on the side of the lane, hand on her hip, striking a pose.

"Don't try to distract me."

"Would I do that?"

"Yeah, I'm thinking you would."

Right now Keera is in last place and it's driving her crazy. I've thought about missing a few pins and letting her creep ahead, but she's pretty competitive and would want a fair game.

I launched my ball down the lane then backed away and watched all ten pins fall.

INSTEAD OF GOING OUT TO A MORE FORMAL DINNER AFTER bowling like we'd originally planned, we decided to just stop into Poor Richard's Pub, which sits right at the entrance to the bowling lanes. Keera took a sip of her beer then plunked the mug down on the table.

"I want a rematch."

"You're such a sore loser," Anjannette said.

"That's not true."

"You literally say you want a rematch every time we come bowling and you lose."

Keera opened her mouth to speak, then closed it. She seemed to think for a minute and instead of offering a rebuttal, took another sip of her beer. Judging by the look on her face, I'm guessing Anjannette isn't exaggerating.

The waitress approached with our food and soon the table was covered with an assortment of platters and baskets of shareable appetizers.

We'd just filled our plates when a couple approached Leo. He stood and shook hands with the man then took a few steps away from the table as the three continued to talk. Anjannette started to eat and I glanced between my plate and Leo a couple times, wondering if I should wait for him to sit.

"You can eat," she said, just loud enough for Keera and me to hear. "That can take a while."

I picked up my fork and speared a chicken wing bite.

"I guess you're used to interruptions like this."

She nodded then gestured between Keera and me.

"It's definitely better when we're with people because he can just do his thing without worrying about leaving me. But honestly, he doesn't get approached when we're out as often as I thought he would."

"That still boggles my mind," Keera said. "Not only because he's a pretty popular player, but also there aren't many MLB players living in Scranton."

"Do you follow baseball?" Anjannette asked me.

I shook my head as I chewed the mozzarella stick I just popped into my mouth.

"Not regularly. My dad is a sports reporter so I usually watch whatever he's covering, but other than that, no."

"Does he work for one of the local news stations?"

Before I could answer, Leo joined us again.

"Sorry about that."

"Never apologize for being a nice guy," Anjannette said, then leaned over and kissed his cheek. "Simon just mentioned that his dad is a sports reporter."

Three sets of eyes turned back to me, so I answered the question Anjannette asked before Leo sat down.

"No, he works for ESPN. He mostly covers football now, but through the years, he's done pretty much everything." I lifted my mug and gestured toward Leo with it. "He interviewed you right when you got moved up to the Waves."

He shifted his eyes from side to side as though he was thinking.

"John Parker?" I nodded. "Oh wow, he's hand's down one of my favorite reporters."

"Yeah, he's great at what he does."

"I never even asked, what's he doing now that he and your mom are traveling?" Keera asked.

"They're both working remotely, but more part time than usual."

I explained my parents' excursion to Anjannette and Leo, which led to a discussion of our bucket list places to visit. Soon the appetizers were gone and our drinks empty.

My phone buzzed in my pocket and I reached down to check the caller ID.

"I apologize. I need to grab this. It's my mom."

I stood and swiped to answer as I headed out of the restaurant.

"Hi mom, what's up?"

"My laptop is acting up. Could you ship my old one out to me?"

"Sure," I said. "What's going on?"

"I don't know. It's really slow starting and shuts down without warning."

My mom knows her way around computers so I didn't take it any farther than that. I'm sure she's done all the basic troubleshooting as well as some more advanced stuff.

"Just text me where you want it shipped and I'll send it out next day air tomorrow."

"I appreciate it," she said. "So, how are things going?"

"Pretty good."

"I'm sorry if I interrupted a date or something, but I have good cell service right now and didn't want to chance not being able to reach you."

Since I didn't mention Keera to my mom, I'm guessing Shannon did. It's not like I date so much that she'd assume that's what I'm doing on a Saturday night.

"Why would you think I'm on a date?"

"I saw that you're at the South Side Lanes, so I'm guessing you're bowling, which isn't something you normally do."

What is it with my mom and sister suddenly stalking my location?

"Actually I'm at Poor Richard's."

"Oh."

I could have left it at that, but figured I'd tell her who I'm with.

"But I am on a date with Keera."

"Simon, you could have just said that."

"I just did."

"So it's going well?"

"So far," I said. "We're on a double date tonight with Keera's friend Anjannette and her fiancé, who just happens to be Leo Marakis. Tell dad."

"He's that adorable baseball player, right?"

"He is a baseball player. I'm not committing to the adorable part."

"I'll be sure to tell him, and I'll text you an address within the hour." she said. "I apologize for interrupting your date."

"It's not a problem."

"And I look forward to meeting Keera when we're home for the holidays."

I hope that will happen too, but I'm just taking this one date at a time right now.

CHAPTER 10

Keera

"I can't believe you have to work all night," I said.

"You know it's easier to do updates when no one else is there."

I'm at the studio late all week, so Simon and I have been Zooming when I get home. But tonight he's doing some kind of system update at work, and since I won't be home before he has to leave for the office, I'm hiding in the corner of the hallway just outside the studio to make the call.

"So you're doing this tonight and tomorrow?"

"If all goes well." He held up his hand with his index and middle finger crossed. "So how's the class planning going?"

"I think we have the basics down, now we're just tweaking it," I said. "The good thing is that once it's done, we won't have to do it again for subsequent classes. For the most part anyway. I'm sure we'll have to change little things as we go along."

"I'm so glad you're doing what you love now. Wilder was

sucking the life out of you."

"Getting laid off was definitely the best thing that ever happened to me, even though it didn't seem like that at the time." I shook my head. "But I don't want to talk about Wilder anymore. Will you be working this weekend?"

"I shouldn't be. What about you?"

"I'm free after three o'clock Friday. Anjannette is doing the Friday night and Saturday classes. And of course, I'm always off on Sunday."

"Would you want to go for a hike Saturday?"

"A hike?" I scrunched my nose. "I can climb a pole, but get me out in the great outdoors and all my muscles abandon me."

"The trail isn't crazy, I promise. There's a windmill park in Bear Creek I think you'll enjoy."

"Like those huge windmills? You get to see them up close?" Simon nodded. "That would be so cool. I'm in."

"It's a date then," he said. "I'll call you tomorrow and we'll set up a time."

We disconnected and I closed my laptop then stood and stretched my legs. Anjannette was just finishing up a beginner class so I stood in the doorway and watched them execute the dance she'd taught them.

Most of the ladies in this class are new to the studio, but I can already see the change in them. Pole helped me feel more comfortable and confident in my body, and I love watching the same transformation in our students. This isn't an easy sport, but for the people who fall in love with it, the rewards are big.

I stepped into the room and clapped as they finished their dance, then walked over to the desk and set my laptop down. Anjannette joined me as the ladies wiped down their poles.

"Did you get Simon?"

"Yeah, I caught him before he left for work." She stared at me and smirked. "What?"

"Nothing," she said. "I just think it's so cute how you were worried you weren't going to get to speak to him tonight."

"I wasn't worried."

"You were panicking."

I rolled my eyes.

"If you say so."

"I do." Her triumphant smile was equal parts annoying and adorable. "You guys really are cute together so I'm glad you're giving it a chance."

"I've never dated someone I was friends with before. It's different, but kind of nice."

We paused our conversation to say goodbye to the students as they left the studio. Which is fine with me. I don't want to dissect or obsessively discuss what's going on with Simon. We're taking things slow and I'm enjoying myself.

Once everyone else left, Anjannette pulled out her notebook and we went through the schedule for the beginners' classes.

"Do you think we should keep the martini spin?" she asked.

"I think everything we have planned is perfect." I reached over and closed her notebook. "Stop obsessing."

"I just want it to go well."

"I do too," I said. "And I think what we have planned is solid. The good thing is that we can alter the plan if necessary. We'll just have to wait and see the skill level of the attendees and take it from there."

"Don't sit there and be the voice of reason when I'm trying to panic," she said with a chuckle.

"Hey, someone has to do it."

"And don't think our Simon conversation is over."

"I'm not sure why. There's not much more to discuss. I like Simon. He's easy to be with and surprisingly, after knowing him for a decade, I'm suddenly attracted to him." I thought about that for a second, then added, "It's not that I thought he was *unattractive*. I always told him what a catch he is. I just never considered catching him myself."

"That's because your hands were always full with the idiots you were dating at the time."

"True."

"So do you plan on breaking your dry spell soon?"

"Honestly, I'm not *planning* anything with this relationship. For the first time, I'm just kind of going with the flow and seeing where we end up."

Simon

"This house is amazing," Keera said as we finished a quick tour. "You grew up here?"

"Yeah, we moved in when Shannon and I were four."

"I would have killed to have a basement like that when I was younger." She leaned against the island. "And the pool. I would have had friends over all the time."

"It was definitely a great place to grow up." I opened the refrigerator and pulled out two brown bags. "Okay, we have a chicken flatbread or tacos."

"First of all, I love the fact that you subscribe to Hello Fresh!," she said. "And second, the answer is always tacos."

I put one of the bags back and closed the door.

"Tacos it is."

I opened the bag and set the ingredients on the counter. "What can I do?"

"Just have a seat so you can watch and marvel at my culinary skills."

I flashed a cheeky smile and held up the recipe card.

She settled onto a stool at the island and rested her elbows on the granite countertop.

"I'm ready to be impressed." She looked at the ingredients. "What's first?"

I've made these before so I have an idea, but glanced at the recipe card anyway.

"Slice and cook the onion."

I pulled a cutting board out of the cupboard and grabbed a knife from the block and got to work.

"I've seen the Hello Fresh! commercials, but never ordered it. It's kind of nice how everything is included."

"Yeah, my mom hated that I ate junk food or takeout all the time, so she gifted me a subscription for Christmas last year." I finished slicing the onion and washed my hands. "It's easy and the food is good, so I kept ordering."

I dried my hands then placed a frying pan on the stovetop and turned on the burner. After drizzling in a small amount of oil, I added the onions.

"You were worried about being able to keep up on the hike, but obviously you shouldn't have been." Picking up a wooden spoon, I stirred the onions around. "You didn't seem to have a problem at all."

"Surprisingly I didn't," she said. "When I hike up to the Top of the World with the pole ladies, I'm always lagging behind. But since we didn't do the whole thing, I think you went easy on me."

"Not really. In my opinion, the miles after the creek are

boring so I prefer to just turn around and hike back out instead of following the loop around. It's a little shorter but the terrain is the same."

We continued to talk about our hike while I browned the ground beef, minced tomato and cilantro, and made the sour cream, lime, and cilantro drizzle. I've never been much of a cook beyond boxed mac and cheese or ramen, but this is just as easy, tastes better, and looks much more impressive.

Once everything was ready, Keera helped me carry the various bowls and plates over to the kitchen table.

"It smells amazing," Keera said as she settled into what's normally Shannon's seat at the table.

I opened the refrigerator and checked the drink options.

"Corona?" I asked.

"Perfect."

I grabbed two bottles, popped off the tops, added a slice of lime to each, and joined her at the table. After handing Keera a bottle, I held mine up and touched it to hers.

"To another great day."

We each took a drink and set our bottles down.

"This looks amazing," she said.

"Then let's dig in."

I watched Keera build a taco then take a bite. She closed her eyes and let out a long, low moan as she chewed. My dick jumped to attention at the sound, making me grateful she can't see through the table.

She opened her eyes and frowned.

"Why aren't you eating?"

Instead of telling her I was imagining the things I'd love to do to her so she'll make that sound again, I said, "Just wanted to make sure you liked them."

"Mmm, they're *so* good."

She popped the last bite into her mouth and chewed as she made another taco.

"What's your schedule look like this week?"

"I have the early classes, so I'll be done by seven. And I'm off Friday night and Saturday again because Anjannette feels guilty that she was gone so much over the summer." She shrugged. "It wasn't a big deal to do all the classes, but I won't turn down the time off, or the spa day she planned for us."

"That's tomorrow, right?"

"Yes, and I'm so looking forward to it."

"Would you like to do something Monday? Maybe a movie or dinner. Or both."

"Sounds good." She wiped her mouth then set the napkin on her plate. "Oh man, I'm stuffed."

"I probably should have told you to save room for peanut butter pie. Maybe you could force down a small slice."

"Give me a little while and I'm sure I'll be up to the task."

She stood and picked up her plate then mine and walked over to place them in the sink. I followed her with the serving bowls and set them on the counter.

"Do you use the dishwasher or just wash by hand?"

"Just set them in the sink. I'll get them later."

"You cooked. I'll wash. Dishwasher or by hand?"

"Dishwasher."

We worked in quiet domesticity. While she filled the dishwasher, I covered the leftovers and placed them in the refrigerator then wiped off the table. It felt so comfortable and I found myself wishing we could do this forever.

"Where's the detergent?"

She opened the cupboard under the sink and bent to

look inside. I walked over and opened the drawer right next to her. She straightened, putting us face-to-face.

We've been together for five hours and other than a quick peck when I first picked her up, I've barely touched her. It's time to remedy that.

Keera's eyes didn't leave mine as I closed the drawer and took a step closer, backing her against the counter. Raising my hand, I cupped her jaw and stroked her cheek with my thumb.

"You are so beautiful." Her gaze didn't leave mine, but her brow furrowed as if my words confused her. That or she doubted them. "You are. You're perfect."

Lowering my head, I sealed our mouths together in a kiss that expressed all my longing and desire. Keera's tongue met mine stroke for stroke, so she must feel the same way. My hands skimmed along her luscious body, enjoying every dip and curve before settling on her breasts and molding them to fit my palm. Our mouths opened and closed over each other as I stroked my thumbs over her nipples in the same steady rhythm.

At some point my brain functioned enough to realize my whole body was leaning against her, pressing her into the counter. I slowly ended the kiss and Keera let out a little mewl of protest then screeched when I placed my hands on her waist and lifted until she was sitting on the counter. Stepping between her wide-spread thighs, I wrapped my arms around her waist and pulled her forward until she was flush against me.

I nibbled at her bottom lip before fully placing my mouth over hers once again. Plowing my fingers through her thick hair, I tilted her head back and to the side, opening her further to my sensual exploration. Keera's fingers curled into my scalp as the kiss went on and on, our tongues twirling in perfect tempo.

Keera loosened her hold on my head, pulled her mouth from mine, and sucked in a breath. I took the opportunity to lean forward and drag my mouth along the column of her perfect neck. Kissing my way down to her collarbone, I nibbled at the pulse breathing wildly at the base of her throat. Her fingers dug into my hair again as I reversed direction and kissed my way back up her neck.

I pulled back just far enough to meet her gaze. Her dilated pupils made her blue eyes look almost black but there was something lingering just beneath the desire.

Taking another step back, I rested my hands on the counter on either side of her hips.

"Keera?"

"Hmm?"

She released my hair and placed her hands on my shoulders.

"Things are getting a little intense here and I'd be more than happy to move somewhere more comfortable. But if you're not ready, that's okay too."

"No, I do want this. So much." She frowned then shook her head. "I just don't think my mind and body are on the same page just yet."

I stepped back and helped her off the counter and interlaced our fingers together.

"Come on, let's go watch a movie."

She blinked up at me, confused at first, then her mouth curled into a smile.

"You may possibly be the most perfect man in the world, Simon Parker."

Leaning forward, I kissed her forehead.

"I won't argue with that."

CHAPTER 11

Keera

"You know, ever since you got engaged to Leo, the bonuses at Peaches & Pole have gotten so much better."

"That's because he makes an insane amount of money to play a game," Anjannette said. "And since I moved in with him, he insists I use *my* money however I wish."

"Well, I'm happy you *wished* to lavish me with a full spa day."

"You deserve it," she said. "*We* deserve it."

"Hell yeah, we do."

I held up my glass of champagne and clinked it against hers before taking a sip.

We started the day in the steam room, then each enjoyed a full-body massage and facial, which included an amazing scalp treatment. Now we're having lunch and when we're done, we'll head downstairs for mani/pedis and blowouts.

"So, are you gonna make me ask?"

"About?"

"Date number three."

"We went hiking on a trail that leads out to the Bear Creek windmills. Those things are huge. It was so cool seeing them up close." I finished my champagne and set the glass down. "Oh, and I didn't have any trouble keeping up like I usually do when we all go hiking. I was very impressed with myself. Teaching pole full time must be whipping me into shape."

Anjannette rested her elbow on the table and leaned forward.

"That's all great and I'm glad you managed to keep up, but you know that's not what I

was asking. I'm curious about what happened *after* the hike."

"We went back to his place and he made tacos."

She sat back, crossed her arms over her chest, and raised her brow. I know what she's asking, I'm just torturing her a little. After all, she never freely offered up details about Leo when they started dating.

"Nothing happened," I said. "I mean, we made out. *A lot.* But that's pretty much it."

"I kind of had the feeling something might happen after our last conversation."

"We were headed there at one point." I scrunched my nose. "I think."

"What do you mean, *you think*?"

"After we ate and cleaned the kitchen, Simon kissed me, and things got pretty intense."

"So what happened? Why'd you stop?"

Before I had to answer, our nail technicians, Ashley and Julia, arrived to escort us downstairs. As I settled into the comfy chair, I thought about Anjannette's question. I won't lie and say I haven't thought about it a million times since

Simon dropped me off last night. But putting all my jumbled thoughts into actual words is going to be tough.

I watched Julia trim and shape my nails, amazed at how much nicer they look when done professionally. My feet are super ticklish, so I fought to stay still as she exfoliated them. She'd just started massaging my calves and feet with vanilla lavender lotion when Anjannette repeated her question.

After shifting my gaze between Julia and Ashley, I mentally shrugged. In their line of work, I'm sure they've heard more interesting things than my lack of sex life. I looked over at Anjannette, who had her whole upper body turned in my direction awaiting my response.

"We cleaned up after dinner, then one thing led to another and we started making out. Things got pretty hot and at one point, he picked me up onto the counter." I shook my head. "I'm still trying to figure out how he managed that."

"Stick to the point," she said.

I took a minute to enjoy the amazing massage Julia was giving my feet, then continued.

"So I'm on the counter and there's a lot of kissing and some heavy petting, and I was all in. So when Simon mentioned moving somewhere more comfortable, I thought I was good with it."

"*Thought?*"

"There was an itty bitty part way in the back of my brain that was second-guessing it. I mean, at this point, I'm sure about Simon, I just don't want to move too fast and screw things up. I want this thing between us to be different."

"Did you tell him all that?"

"No, but somehow he knew. Maybe not everything going through my head, but he knew I was having doubts and he stopped. Then he told me it's okay if I'm not ready and we went into the living room and watched *Hocus Pocus*."

Julia finished painting my toenails and I looked down to check them out.

"I love them. Thanks so much."

The orange with black polka dots are perfect for this time of year and will look great in the spooky photo shoot we're doing at the studio this week. My manicure will match with my ring fingers painted black with orange polka dots as accent nails.

We all headed over to the manicure area and Anjannette and I sat next to each other.

"And that was it?" she asked while Julia and Ashley worked on our cuticles.

"For the most part. We made out a little more on the couch, but it didn't get as heated as in the kitchen." I shrugged. "Then he took me home."

"Definitely a change from all the other guys you dated."

"For sure," I said. "I think that was the first time I didn't feel like I *had* to have sex. You

know?"

"I do know, and I felt the same way with Leo. It just goes to show how wrong the guys we used to date were for us."

"It's so obvious now. Why did I waste so many years on losers?"

"Hindsight is always twenty-twenty," she said. "Do you and Simon have plans to go out again?"

"Yeah, we're going to dinner tomorrow night."

"And what are you thinking about that?"

I watched Julia place tiny black dots on my thumb nail. There's been so much running through my head since Simon dropped me off last night, but there's one thing I know.

"I want to take things to the next level tomorrow night." I looked over at Anjannette. "I'm ready."

Simon

I took one last look at the selfie Keera sent me of her at the spa and replied with a hot emoji. She looks adorable wearing the fluffy robe, but I'm guessing she's naked underneath and the thought of that is definitely hot.

I've seen her wearing nothing but a pole top and shorts, so I know how amazing her curves look, but last night I got to really touch and explore them. And it was incredible.

It was tough releasing her, but it was obvious to me that she had doubts about taking things further. And I don't want any doubt in her mind, no matter how small, the first time we have sex.

Settling onto the couch, I clicked on the TV and scrolled through the channels. Before I found something to watch, my phone buzzed. I picked it up and saw Shannon's name on caller ID. My sister is the last person I expected to be calling. She usually goes to brunch then hangs out with her friends on Sundays.

"Hey Shan."

"Hey."

"Everything okay?"

"Yeah." She sighed. "I just wanted to let you know that I'll be home next weekend."

"Shower? Birthday party?"

"No, nothing is going on. I just feel like getting out of the city."

I sat forward and rested my elbows on my knees.

"Everything okay?" I asked again.

This time, it took her a little longer to answer.

"We'll talk when I get home. I'll see you Thursday night."

"See you then."

Something has definitely been going on with Shannon the past few months, but whatever it is, she hasn't wanted to talk about it. Maybe this weekend she will.

I picked up the remote and scrolled again, happy when I found an *It's Always Sunny in Philadelphia* marathon. I'd just finished watching one episode when the doorbell rang. That reminded me that Andrew and Archer were coming over today. Between Keera's text and Shannon's call, I'd gotten totally distracted and forgot.

"Hey guys," I said as I opened the door.

"You have Mountain Dew, right?" Archer asked as he walked across the threshold.

"I believe so."

Andrew followed him carrying a tray of pizza with a container on top, which I assume holds chicken wings.

"They didn't have any at the pizza shop and Andrew wouldn't stop anywhere else."

"Because I told you Simon usually has it."

"*Usually* isn't always."

I followed them into the kitchen and opened the drink refrigerator, breathing a sigh of relief when I spotted four cans of Mountain Dew on the bottom shelf.

"Stop bickering children, I have some. What do you want, Andrew?"

He looked over and decided on a beer. I grabbed the drinks and set them on the island, then took a seat. They've spent enough time here and know where everything is kept and already set out paper plates and napkins. I grabbed one of each then took a slice.

"How was hiking yesterday?" Andrew asked then looked me over as he took a sip of beer. "It doesn't look like anything is scraped, sprained, or broken so that's a plus."

"Very funny." I took a bite of pizza and chewed. "You act like I've never gone hiking before."

"I know you have because I put the cast on your wrist after one of your hiking trips a few years ago."

"I hurt myself *one time* and I have to hear about it forever."

"Don't forget about that time in junior high when you ended up in the emergency room with all those bee stings," Archer said.

"How is it my fault that I got swarmed by bees?"

"I didn't say it was your fault. It's just a fact."

Shaking my head, I finished my slice and reached for some chicken wings.

"But to answer your question, our hike was nice."

"I'll never understand the appeal of being outdoors, especially in the woods," Archer said. "I hope you checked yourselves for ticks."

I'm not even gonna comment on that.

"Speaking of outdoors," Andrew said, thankfully changing the subject. "If you guys aren't doing anything Saturday afternoon, there are bands playing all day at Nay Aug Park."

"Shannon is coming home Thursday, so I'm actually not sure what I'm doing next weekend."

"Thursday?" Archer asked. "Does that mean game night is cancelled?"

"I'll let you know. It depends on what she's doing."

"We could just order in and hang out instead of gaming."

This from Andrew, who's had a crush on my sister since the first time he laid eyes on her back in Kindergarten. I'm pretty sure he started hanging around with me back in the day just to get close to her. Even now, he tries to be available anytime she's home. Unfortunately for him, she put him firmly in the friend zone years ago.

Then again, Keera put me there years ago and look at us now. So I guess there's always hope. There are definitely worse people Shannon could end up with.

"I'll see what Shannon is up to and let you know later in the week."

CHAPTER 12

Keera

"I'M NOT SURE WHAT SHANNON HAS GOING ON, BUT IF SHE'S not doing anything with her friends while she's here this weekend, maybe we can all do something."

Simon and I had finished eating dinner and were just waiting for the check. For the last few minutes he's been telling me how he thinks something is going on with Shannon. I'm sympathetic to the fact he's concerned about his sister, but part of my mind is occupied thinking about what I hope is going to happen once we leave here.

"Sure, that'll be fun."

The waitress finally brought the check. Simon handed her his credit card and she swiped it through a handheld reader. After he signed the receipt, we were on our way.

Simon had picked me up at the studio, which is in the opposite direction of his house, so I have to let him know what I'm thinking before we pull out of the parking lot. He settled behind the wheel and as he started the engine, I shifted in my seat to face him.

"So I was thinking..." He raised his eyebrows as I trailed off. "I'd really like to see your house again." His eyebrows rose even higher as his mouth formed a perfect O as my meaning set in. "If that's okay."

"That's–sure. Great."

He held the wheel with a white-knuckled grip and pulled out of the parking lot. We didn't speak on the short drive to his house, but it wasn't an awkward silence. It was more charged and filled with anticipation.

Simon turned into his driveway, opened the garage door, and pulled inside. After shutting the engine off, he closed the door behind us, then stepped out of the car. He walked around and opened my door, then held out his hand to help me out. I kept hold of it as we walked inside.

As we entered the kitchen, he turned to face me.

"Would you like a drink?" I shook my head and he took a step toward me. "What would you like?"

My lady parts tingled at the deep timbre of his voice.

"I was hoping we could pick up where we left off Saturday night." I rested my hand against his chest. "Except maybe we could head to your room instead of starting here."

"Are you sure?"

I nodded and moved closer until my chest pressed against his. A slow, sexy smile spread across his face, but I only had a second to appreciate it before he grabbed my hand and pulled me toward the stairs.

Simon let go of my hand at the threshold of his room and walked inside to turn on a lamp. It provided a soft glow and I took a step forward, taking in my surroundings. The masculine colors give the room a cozy feel and I made a mental note to check out the books and collectibles neatly displayed on the wall of shelves later.

He walked over and took both of my hands in his.

"You still sure?"

I don't remember any of the guys I've been with before asking me that. Much less twice in five minutes.

"I'm positive."

Simon lowered his head and sealed our mouths together. I slipped my arms around his neck, matching his longing and desire with each bold kiss. He wrapped his arms around my waist and pulled me up onto my tiptoes, bringing me tighter against him. With our mouths still fused together, he took slow, deliberate steps backward, moving us toward the bed.

I curled my fingers into his hair as our tongues tangled, the kiss going on for what seemed like forever. Not that I'm complaining. Making out is one of my favorite things, and Simon is an excellent kisser.

He pulled his mouth from mine, allowing me to suck in a much-needed breath. Goosebumps trailed over my body as he kissed his way down my neck and nibbled at a spot behind my ear. How did he know that would drive me crazy when I had no idea?

His lips skimmed along my jaw to my chin and moved to the other side, giving it the same treatment. I rubbed my nipples against his chest, hoping to give them some relief, but it just made them ache even more. Is it possible to come just from this? I never would have thought so, but at this point, it wouldn't take much to push me over the edge.

My hips bucked forward at that thought, pressing against what feels like a pretty impressive erection. His hands shifted to my ass and squeezed, holding me in place as he thrust against me. I heard his low moan against my ear a second before he closed his teeth over the lobe and tugged. He pulled back and met my gaze. He's wearing his contacts tonight and his green eyes are dark with passion.

Shifting his hold, he curled his fingers into the material of my dress and slowly inched it up. I stepped back as he pulled it over my head, leaving me standing in front of him in a blue bra and panty set. It's one of my favorites. The lace detail gives what would be a plain cotton set a sexy flair.

Simon's eyes took a lazy tour of my body as he tossed the dress to the floor behind him.

"You're so beautiful."

His low, reverent tone brought tears to my eyes and I blinked them away. Now is not the time for my new-found sappiness to rear its head.

He placed his hands on either side of my face, his thumbs lightly stroking my cheeks.

"Everything okay?" he asked.

I took in a deep breath and nodded. I've never been this nervous before sex, not even my first time. And I'm not nervous in an I-don't-want-to-do-this kind of way. It's more of an I-know-nothing-will-be-the-same-after-this thing.

"This is just..." I trailed off, trying to think of a word to describe what I'm feeling. "More. Special. And to be honest, kind of intense."

I nibbled at my bottom lip and Simon's eyes shifted to my mouth before meeting my gaze again.

"This is perfect." He flashed a smile that was equal parts sexy and sweet. "Just like you."

As he stepped forward, I was forced to step back until the back of my thighs rested against the bed. He shifted his hands from my face to my hips and pressed me down onto the soft mattress. I kicked off my shoes and rested one foot on the edge of the bed and moved back toward the middle.

Simon brushed his fingertips across my abdomen then rested his knee next to me and leaned down, trailing his lips along the same path. He nipped at my navel before continuing upward. Through the soft cotton of my bra, he teased my nipple with his tongue, before drawing it into the moist heat of his mouth. Our eyes held as he ran his tongue around it ever so slowly, spiraling toward the center. His cheeks hollowed as he sucked. My back arched as I let out a long, low moan. He reached around, and very impressively released the fastener of my bra one-handed.

Cool air brushed against my heated skin as he backed away to remove my bra. But he was back before I could protest, his body pressing mine into the mattress as we devoured each other, our lips and tongues stroking, tasting, and savoring.

The soft cotton of his shirt brushed against my tight nipples and I wanted to feel him skin-on-skin. I moved my hands down his body, then back up, dragging his T-shirt with them. Our kiss ended just long enough for him to pull it over his head.

I caught sight of a light dusting of coppery brown hair on his chest before he settled between my thighs and I felt it against my naked torso. The coarse hair brushed my overly-sensitive nipples as he moved over me, taking my mouth in another panty-melting kiss.

Sliding his hands around and down, he gripped my ass and pulled me against the ridge of his erection and thrust forward. After the third time, he ripped his mouth from mine and sucked in a sharp breath. The combination of that and the heated look in his eyes sent a delicious shiver down my spine.

I let out a mewl of protest when he shifted back onto his knees.

"We need to move this forward before I totally lose it," he said, flashing a strained smile.

Hooking his fingers into the waistband of my panties, he backed away just enough to pull them down my legs. After tossing them to the floor, he leaned forward and kissed the arch of my foot, then my knee before deliberately inching his way up my thigh, alternately kissing and nibbling on the way up.

When he settled between my thighs and opened his mouth over their juncture, I nearly jumped off the bed. Simon placed a restraining hand on my belly as his hot gaze met mine over the expanse of my body.

He licked, nipped, and sucked until I was hovering on the edge. When his tongue slid over my clit, I tangled my fingers in his hair and said his name, but it came out more as a low moan.

"Hmmm?"

That sound vibrated through me and I moaned again. I caught a glimpse of his devilish smile as he did it again, eliciting the same response from me.

I didn't think it could get any better but then he slipped his middle finger into my slick folds and began a steady in and out motion while his tongue circled the tiny nub of nerves. My hips thrust up, keeping the rhythm he'd set as his index finger joined in the game.

Any thought of making this last was shot to hell when he opened his mouth over my clit and sucked. All the pleasure concentrated in that magic spot then burst through my entire body.

"Simon."

My desperate voice echoed off the walls and I dug my fingers into his shoulders as the waves went on and on.

Simon stayed with me, his hands moving over and in me with soothing strokes.

"That was incredible," I said when I could finally speak.

His mouth curled up into an adorable smile as he pushed back onto his knees. My eyes shifted to his bare chest and flat abdomen. He usually wears baggy clothes that don't hint at the lean muscle underneath. I followed his happy trail down to what looks like an impressive bulge in his jeans. I sat up and ran my fingertips over his stomach, but he grabbed my hands when I reached his waistband.

"I'm ready to burst. If you touch me in any way, shape, or form, I'm going to seriously embarrass myself here," he said with a strained chuckle.

"Okay, then you do it."

I rested back on my elbows and waited. He stood and removed his jeans and underwear in one swipe. His dick bobbed up against his stomach. *Way up.*

"Holy shit." My eyes widened before reluctantly leaving the impressive sight to meet his gaze. "*That* dick was in the office next to me for more than a decade and I had no idea?"

The corner of his mouth kicked up at my words, but the smile looked strained. I can't even imagine how he's feeling. Even after that amazing orgasm, I want more. Especially after seeing what he's packing.

He turned and retrieved a foil packet from the bedside table. I held my breath and watched as he ripped it open and rolled the condom down his spectacular length.

Placing his knee on the bed again, he leaned down and rested his hands on either side of my head and gave me a quick kiss.

"This is going to be really fast, but I promise, I'll make it up to you next time."

That said, he moved between my legs and plunged

inside. I lifted my hips to meet his every thrust as he pumped in and out in a mind-blowing rhythm.

"Keera," he said, his voice a mere rasp in my ear.

Wanting to feel more, needing to feel more, I wrapped my legs around his waist. Simon gripped my ass and tilted my hips. The new position had his pelvis pressing against my clit with each forward thrust.

That did it.

I let out a long, hoarse moan as I came for the second time in less than five minutes. Some part of my brain registered the fact that Simon had let out his own shout just before he collapsed on top of me.

SIMON

IF MY HEART STOPPED BEATING NOW, I'D DIE A HAPPY MAN. Since puberty, I fantasized about being with a female in this room, but what just happened between Keera and me surpassed every single one of them.

"What are you thinking about?"

I chuckled and she moved her head from my chest to my bicep to look me in the eye.

"I was thinking that it was worth waiting thirty-two years to finally have a girl in this room."

"Thirty-two years, huh?"

"Let's say twenty. I wasn't that interested in girls the first twelve years."

"So we just christened your room?"

"I guess we did."

"Cool."

She kissed my shoulder then pushed up onto her elbow and looked across the room.

"Those are some pretty impressive shelves."

I groaned and rubbed my hand down my face.

"Go ahead, get the busting out of the way."

"What? I'm being serious. It looks like you have some stellar stuff over there. If I wasn't naked, I'd go get a closer look."

"Don't let me stop you. I won't mind at all."

She pinched my waist then settled back against my chest.

"I'll check it out later. This bed is so comfy." She rubbed her cheek against my chest. "Or maybe it's just you."

I kissed the top of her head, amazed at how natural this feels. After sex can be so awkward, especially the first time. But there's none of that with Keera. Maybe it's because we were friends for so long, or maybe it's just because we're meant to be together. I realize how ridiculous that last thought sounds after just a handful of dates, but my feelings for her started a long time before our relationship did.

"Do you have more?"

"More what?"

"Collectibles and books."

"There might be a few dozen boxes in the attic."

"A few dozen?"

My chin brushed against her hair as I nodded.

"But those are the things I used to play with all the time. They're not as pretty."

"I bet they're more loved though."

"They're loved in a different way."

"I'm guessing you have some pretty cool stuff."

"I think so," I said. "But not everyone does."

"Well *I* do. You know I'm a nerdy gothic girl at heart, right?"

"The fact that you call them collectibles instead of dolls tells me everything I need to know."

"Who calls them dolls?"

"Shannon," I said. "She calls me Andy."

"Like in the *The 40-Year-Old Virgin*?"

"Exactly."

"That's actually kind of funny." She looked up at me. "No offense."

I kissed the tip of her nose, then her lips.

"None taken."

Before settling her head back against my chest, she glanced toward the nightstand and smiled.

"What was that smile for?"

"It's only ten-thirty. I thought it was a lot later." She rested her cheek against my chest. "I'm not ready to leave yet. It's too snuggly in this bed."

I rubbed my hand up and down her back then rested it on her hip.

"You don't have to leave at all."

Keera leaned back to look at me and I shifted onto my side to better face her.

"Really?"

I nodded.

"Unless you need to get home."

"I'd love to stay." I felt the *but* coming before she said it. "But I should get home. I wouldn't want Granny Vi to worry if she wakes up in the middle of the night and I'm not there." She nibbled at her bottom lip. "I could text her. Even if she doesn't see it right now, it'll be there if she does wake up."

"No, that's okay. I wouldn't want her to worry." I tucked her hair behind her ear. "We'll plan better next time."

"Next time?"

She slid her leg over my hip and shifted closer. I looked up at the ceiling and crossed my middle and index fingers.

"Please let there be a next time."

Her answering laugh made me smile.

"After what I experienced tonight, you can bet your ass there will be." She raised her brows. "In fact, I don't have to leave just yet. We can have an initial next time to hold us over until the real one."

Reaching out, I wrapped my hands around her waist and pulled her in for a quick kiss. At least the first one was quick. The second was long, slow, wet, and deep.

I'm a huge fan of kissing and Keera seems to enjoy it as much as I do. My erection pressed against her stomach as I continued to feast on her mouth. On and on the kiss went until we needed to pull apart to take in some air.

I released her mouth and after taking a deep breath, I rolled Keera onto her back and settled between her thighs. Nibbling my way down her neck, I licked at the pulse pounding at its base before making my way downward. Before I reached her perfect breasts, she curled her fingers into my hair and directed my attention back up to her face.

"I think it's my turn to explore."

I couldn't help but smile at both her words and the sexy tone she used. Rolling onto my back, I leaned against my pillow and spread my arms out wide before tucking them beneath my head.

"I'm all yours."

CHAPTER 13

Keera

I UNLOCKED THE DOOR AND STEPPED INTO THE STUDIO. AFTER setting my bag on the desk, I turned on all the lights and looked around. It's always strange being here alone. There's so much energy when the room is full of students, not to mention noise. Without that, it feels like a different space. But I'm going to fill it with my own energy right now. It's been a while since I danced just for myself, but I woke up itching to get on the pole.

My least favorite part of dancing is the warmup beforehand, but it's a necessary evil. I turned on my workout playlist and got to it. After jogging around the studio a few times, I did some squats, lunges, and push-ups, then finished with floor stretches.

Feeling sufficiently warm, I stripped off my leggings then sat on the floor to put on my knee pads and heels. I don't have any specific choreography planned, I'm just going to freestyle and let my body move the way it wants. And I know the exact song I want to dance to today.

The clicking of my heels echoed through the room as I walked over to my computer and found "Love on the Brain" by Rhianna. As the first strains of the song began, I grabbed the closest pole and moved my hips, swaying to the slow, sexy rhythm. As she started to sing, I did a step-around, followed by a pirouette that ended with me facing the pole and flowing right into body waves.

Another quick pirouette put my back against the pole. Keeping my grip high, I lifted my right leg and straightened it in front of me as I slid to the floor. Low flow is my jam and once I got down there, I lost myself in the music, crawling and thrusting and rolling, my hands stroking over my body and through my hair.

A forward roll brought me back to the pole and I shifted to my knees and moved up and down in slow, sultry waves. I feel sexy and empowered and more content than I've been in a long time, if ever.

I grabbed the pole and swung my leg around, spinning up to stand. Climbing to the middle of the pole, I shifted into a pole sit, then squeezed my thighs together and bent my legs. I caught a glimpse of myself in the mirror as I held my arms out on either side and smiled. I look like a large bird trying to fly.

The song was coming to an end and I kept watching as I loosened my thighs and dropped down the pole. I tightened them again just before I reached the floor and folded forward into an emotional ball. Before setting my feet on the ground, I hung there for a second to catch my breath. I just stood when I heard clapping. Thankfully I was still holding onto the pole and was able to keep from falling off my heels when I jumped at the noise.

I glanced up and found Anjannette leaning against the wall, with a big smile on her face.

"You scared the shit out of me."

"That. Was. Amazing."

"Thanks," I said as I took off my heels. "But you still scared me."

She settled onto the couch as I picked up a spray bottle and rag and wiped down the pole. Once I was done, I sat in the chair across from her.

"I obviously wasn't going to let you know I was here. You either would have stopped or held back what you were doing. And that dance was so raw and in the moment, I didn't want anything to disrupt its beauty and power. So I let you keep expressing yourself without interruption."

I reached over and grabbed a scrunchie out of my bag and pulled my hair into a messy bun.

"I woke up this morning dying to dance. It's been a long time since I freestyled like that. It felt good."

"Any particular reason you woke up feeling so..." She trailed off and gestured with her hands, her brows raised. "*Inspired*?"

My mouth curled up into a slow smile and I shrugged.

"Maybe."

"Oh my God! You're blushing!"

Anjannette stared at me with her mouth open then she let out a loud *whoop* and jumped up from the couch to give me a big hug.

"I'm so happy for you." She pulled back. "How was it?"

Apparently my smile was enough of an answer. She screeched and squeezed me again before settling back onto the couch.

"I'm so happy for you," she said again.

I sat forward, removed my knee pads, and slipped them

into my bag, trying to figure out what to say about what happened between Simon and me last night. We always tease each other asking about details, but we've never shared specifics, just the general feels.

"It was so much more than anything I've ever experienced." I looked her in the eye. "Anjannette, I think I could really fall for him."

She smirked.

"And *I think* you already have."

I placed my head in my hands and groaned.

"What's wrong?" she asked. "This is a good thing."

"I know. It's just scary."

It was easier to say that last sentence with my face covered.

"Trust me when I say, I totally understand. You know how freaked out I was when I realized I was falling in love with Leo, and look how that turned out."

I lowered my hands and looked over at her.

"This thing with Simon is just *more*. All my prior relationships had a kind of angsty undertone. I never felt like I could one hundred percent be myself, you know?"

"Oh, I definitely know."

"Simon is so sweet, and the way he looks at me..." I shook my head as I trailed off. "When Brian looked at me, I always felt like he was judging me, or making a mental list of my flaws. But Simon makes me feel beautiful."

"That's the way it should be."

I heard the door to the building open, then voices sounded in the hallway.

"I didn't realize the time."

"It flies when you're having fun," she said as few of the ladies for the five-thirty class

walked through the door.

I stood and walked over to the desk to check them in.

"Before I forget," Anjannette said once I was done. "Leo rented out Electric City Axe Throwing Saturday night. Would you and Simon want to come along?"

"He rented the *whole* place?"

She nodded and rolled her eyes.

"He *says* it's so we have an uninterrupted night out, but personally I think it's because he's never thrown an axe before and doesn't want to embarrass himself."

"I agree with your assessment," I said. "I'll check with Simon. His sister is coming home for the weekend and he mentioned possibly doing something with her."

"Bring her along. After all, we have the *whole* place."

SIMON

MY CELL BUZZED AND I OPENED MY EYES, DISORIENTED. Grabbing the phone off the coffee table, I smiled when I saw Keera's name on the caller ID.

"Hey." I cleared my throat. "Hi."

"I'm so sorry. Did I wake you up?" Keera asked.

"I just dozed off watching TV. No worries."

"Sorry I'm so late. I thought I would have been home earlier, but a few of the ladies wanted some ideas for their recital dances and I lost track of time."

I shifted to a sitting position and dragged my fingers through my hair.

"It's not even ten o'clock, you have nothing to be sorry about. I'm actually glad I woke up because otherwise I'd be awake in the middle of the night," I said. "How was your day?"

"Good. I ran some errands with Granny Vi in the morning then we went out for lunch. I woke up itching to dance, so I went to the studio early."

"Did you enjoy yourself?

"I did. It felt so good to just move. Since I started working at the studio full time, all my effort has been put into teaching classes. It was nice to dance for myself."

"I've never seen you dance."

"Do you want to?"

"Hell yeah."

"You'll have to buy a ticket to the recital."

I heard the smile in her voice.

"When is it?"

"The first Saturday in December."

"I'll be there."

The fact that she's talking about something more than a month away is a good sign that things between us have changed since last night. Before, we took it one day at a time. I'm thrilled that things are at a new level.

"Just a warning," she said. "My schedule will be crazy next month when everyone really starts practicing."

"Hopefully you'll find time to fit me in."

"Definitely, but you might have to be a little flexible."

"I'll start taking yoga."

Keera laughed at my pathetic joke and it ended on a yawn.

"Sorry, it's been a long day."

"I guess neither of us got much sleep last night, but I don't have any regrets about that."

"Me neither."

"I'm very happy to hear it."

A charged silence zinged through the phone line. I kind of wish I asked Keera to come over when she was done at the studio, but that would have been selfish. Like I said, neither of us got much sleep last night so it's for the best that we get some tonight.

"Last night was amazing, Simon. I really had a great time."

"I did too. Maybe we can get together tomorrow night and discuss it some more?"

"Hmm, I think I'd rather get together and maybe *do* it some more."

My laugh echoed through the room.

"That's even better than what I had in mind."

"What did you have in mind?"

"Dinner."

"I'll be done at the studio at seven, so we can fit in both."

"Sounds like a plan."

"Now that we have that sorted," she said. "Anjannette told me that Leo is renting out Electric City Axe Throwing Saturday night and asked if we want to go along. I mentioned that we might be doing something with Shannon and she said to bring her along."

"I spoke with her earlier and she's not making plans with her friends, so she'll definitely be around. Are other people going?"

"I'm not sure. Why?"

"She may not want to go if it's just the five of us."

"I'll ask Anjannette tomorrow," she said. "I'm really looking forward to spending some time with Shannon. I plan on hearing all your embarrassing stories."

"I'm sure she's looking forward to telling you all of them," I said. "Just remember that turnabout is fair play. You have a brother who I'm sure would love to fill me in on you."

"I'm sure my whole family would love to fill you in."

"That's something to look forward to." She yawned again and I figured it was time to hang up. "I'll let you go so you can get to sleep. I'll pick you up at the studio at seven?"

"Why don't you make one of your Hello Fresh! meals and I'll come over when I'm done at the studio?"

"Are you sure?"

"Positive."

CHAPTER 14

Keera

"Well hello Paul Bunyan."

I stuck my tongue out at Granny Vi and flopped onto the couch.

"Very funny."

"Where are you headed looking like a lumberjack?"

"Axe throwing." I glanced down at my jeans, white T-shirt, and unbuttoned plaid flannel shirt. "Do I really look bad?"

"You look fine. I'm just having some fun," she said. "Are you going to be in the woods? Will you be warm enough?"

"No, it's inside. We're going to Electric City Axe Throwing."

I sat on the couch to put on my boots.

"There's a place you go to throw an axe?"

"Yep."

"What do you throw the axe at?"

"I've never been, but from what I saw online, you throw at a big piece of wood with a bullseye painted on it."

"What will they come up with next?" She shook her head. "Are just the two of you going?"

"No, Leo rented out the whole place, so we're tagging along with him, Anjannette, and whoever else shows up. Simon's sister Shannon is visiting for the weekend, so she's coming along too."

"So you're spending time with Simon's sister but can't bring him around your family?" She crossed her arms over her chest. "Hmmph, I see how it is."

"First of all, it's just Simon's sister, not his whole flipping family. And it's not like you haven't met him. Second, I'm thirty-two years old. Does my entire family need to meet every guy I date at this point in my life?"

"I met him for a few minutes when he picked you up that one day, but your parents and brother didn't. And I don't think your age has anything to do with it. You're spending a lot of time with this boy and it seems as if you like him. What are you gonna do, invite us to the wedding when the time comes and have us meet him there?"

I rolled my eyes and sighed. I'm not going to win this. Besides, even though we've only been together a few weeks, I think it's safe to say that Simon and I have moved beyond dating and into a relationship. So it's not out of the question that I should introduce him to my family.

Plus, he's not like the other guys I've dated, thankfully. My family's love language is busting ass and I was always worried they'd offend my exes. Like Granny Vi said, they were all "tall and muscular with a fragile ego." Simon is much more secure and I don't think harmless teasing will freak him out too much.

"Okay, let's set something up. What are you thinking?"

I'm sure I shocked her by agreeing so easily, but she didn't show it.

"Bring him to dinner tomorrow."

"So soon?"

"Why not? It's not a test. He doesn't need to study."

"I'll see what's going on with his sister."

"Bring her too. We'll all get to know each other."

"Don't get too far ahead of yourself," I said.

Before she could comment, the doorbell rang. I stood and opened the door and found Simon standing there, dressed similar to me, except his flannel shirt is blue.

"Nice outfit," I said.

His gaze skimmed down my body, then up before meeting mine again.

"It looks *much* better on you."

He leaned forward and gave me a quick kiss. Before I could say anything, Granny Vi's voice came from directly behind me.

"Simon, I want you and your sister to come to dinner tomorrow."

I stepped back and looked at my grandmother. She very obviously avoided looking at my face.

"Oh, okay," he said. "I'm not sure what time Shannon's leaving, but I'd love to come."

"Perfect. Dinner is at four, but you can come over anytime." Her eyes shifted between us. "In fact, instead of bringing Keera home in the wee hours of the morning, you can just sleep in and get here sometime after noon."

Simon's eyes rounded. I'm sure he has no idea how to respond to that.

"On that note, we're gonna head out," I said.

After grabbing my purse, I ushered him out the door.

"Bye Mrs. Jordan," he said before I closed it.

"See you tomorrow, Simon."

Simon

"Isn't Shannon coming?" Keera asked when I settled behind the wheel.

"She's driving herself over."

Keera made a sound acknowledging my answer but didn't say anything more. I started the car and pulled onto the street.

"I'm sorry about Granny Vi."

"Sorry about what?"

"She kind of bulldozed you into dinner," she said. "And also for the sleeping-in comment."

"That comment was harmless, and I didn't feel bulldozed. Dinner will be fun."

She snorted.

"Just be forewarned, my family tosses sarcasm around like confetti."

Keera dated two different guys in the ten years we worked together, and many Monday mornings were filled with her telling me about how some snarky comment one of her family members made upset them. Honestly, I never thought anything said warranted more than a chuckle, but her guys had trouble handling it.

I turned into the parking lot of Electric City Axe Throwing, pulled into a spot, and turned off the engine. After releasing my seatbelt, I shifted to face Keera.

"Your family doesn't scare me. I grew up with Shannon."

She chuckled at that last sentence, and looked a little relieved.

I gave her what was supposed to be a quick peck, but Keera bit my bottom lip as I started to pull away then opened her mouth over mine. Our tongues tangled and tasted, and I wrapped my arms around her waist, pulling her closer to deepen the kiss. I only got to enjoy that for a second when someone banged on my window.

Jumping back, I released Keera and looked over my shoulder. Shannon stood just outside my door with a big smile on her face, waving. I flipped her off and turned back to Keera.

"See what I mean?"

She glanced over my shoulder and a big smile spread across her face.

"You just might be okay with my family."

KEERA TOOK ANOTHER SLICE OF PIZZA FOR HERSELF AND placed one on my plate, too.

"Thank you."

I kissed her cheek, then picked up the pizza and took a bite.

We'd all taken several tries at throwing axes, some with more success than others. Aside from Leo and Anjannette, three women from the pole studio are also here, Eve, Sophie, and Phoebe, who brought her boyfriend Josh. The latter two ate quickly then went upstairs to play the digital game targets. At least that's what they said. I haven't heard any noise up there, so I'll just make it a point to stay down here.

"I can't believe this place is BYOB," Anjannette said, then took a drink of beer.

"Yeah, I wouldn't think alcohol and throwing an axe mix well," Eve agreed.

"Which is why I only got a twelve pack," Leo said.

"Maybe it'll help me actually hit the target," Keera said then looked at Shannon who'd hit the bullseye nine times out of ten. "What's your secret?"

Shannon finished chewing the bite she'd just taken then swallowed.

"Well, it helps that I've done this before. Once you find the rhythm, it's pretty easy." She took a drink. "It also helps when you need to blow off a little steam. You give the throw an extra oomph that's needed to really slam it into the wood."

"That's true," Eve said. And from what I saw, she hit the target about half the time. "I also pictured my ex-husband's face on the bullseye." She stood. "In fact, I'm gonna go hit it a few more times. It's better than therapy."

"I don't have the same rage at my ex-husband, but I'll agree, throwing the axe is definitely therapeutic." Sophie said. "I think I'll join you."

We watched them walk toward the cages, then Leo turned back to the table.

"Ouch," he said. "Remind me never to piss you ladies off."

"You don't have to worry, I'm not picturing your face." Anjannette squeezed his bicep.

"Would you show me the secret to hitting the target?" Keera asked Shannon, then she looked at me. "I won't picture your face either. I promise."

"Sure." Shannon finished her beer and stood. "Let's go."

"I'm coming too," Anjanette said as she scrambled out of her seat and followed them across the room.

Leo finished eating then started tossing empty paper

plates and napkins into one of the empty pizza boxes. I gathered up the empty bottles and tossed them into the recycling bin. As we finished clearing the table, loud bangs sounded from the axe cages.

"I'm not sure if we want to go near them," Leo said with a chuckle.

Whatever technique Shannon showed them helped, because each woman was hitting her target with every throw.

"This is much more fun than what I was doing before," Keera said. "Hey, let's all do it at the same time."

The others agreed and each woman stepped up to the line at the back of her cage. After counting down from five, they synchronized their throws and a second later, their axes slammed into the wood.

They jumped up and down and cheered. My eyes shifted from Keera to Shannon. I know when my sister is going through the motions, and that's what she's doing now. We'll have to talk before she leaves tomorrow.

CHAPTER 15

Keera

"Why are you home?" Granny Vi asked as I walked into the kitchen.

"Good morning to you, too."

I pulled a mug from the cupboard and filled it with coffee. After adding vanilla-flavored creamer, I joined her at the table.

"I figured you'd be at Simon's."

"Shannon is there and he wanted to talk to her about something, so he just brought me home after axe throwing."

Plus their rooms are right next to each other and I didn't want to test the thickness of the walls. But Granny Vi doesn't need to know that.

"How was axe throwing?"

"It was so much fun. You and your friends should go."

"We'd probably hurt ourselves."

"We all got out unscathed." I flexed my fingers and rolled my neck. "Although my hands hurt and my shoulders are kind of sore. Which is weird, considering what I do for a living. You'd think they'd be more conditioned."

"My friends and I will stick to the casino and going out to dinner."

"Your loss." I stood and walked over to the counter. "I'm gonna make some toast. Do you want any?"

"No thanks, I already ate."

I popped two slices of bread into the toaster then leaned against the counter.

"What are you making for dinner?"

"Roast beef, mashed potatoes, and corn. Your mom is bringing brownies and stuff to make them à la mode."

"Yummy."

"I also got some National hard rolls. Simon eats normal, right?"

"He does."

"Thank the good Lord. Having the last one to dinner gave me a headache."

In the last couple years of our relationship, Brian was always following some special diet or another. Keto, Paleo, Macro counting, intermittent fasting...you name it, he did it. And I agree with Granny Vi, it gave me a headache, too. Just when I got used to one, he'd change.

I pulled my toast out of the toaster and sat back down. After spreading raspberry jelly on both slices, I picked up one and took a bite.

"What time are you starting dinner?" I asked after I finished the first slice.

"Around two."

"After I eat this, I'm going to head back to bed for a couple hours, but I'll be out in time to help you."

"You feeling okay?"

"Yeah, it's just been a long week and I think it's finally catching up with me."

She raised her brow.

"You're not pregnant, are you?"

"No I'm not pregnant." I shook my head. "In fact, I'm probably getting my period soon. I'm bloated and I've been tired all week."

"I don't miss that."

"I could definitely live without it, but I'll take *it* over a baby."

"Now that you're in a relationship with a normal man, you might change your mind about that."

"Maybe, but that's way off."

"Not necessarily. I only dated your grandfather four months before we got engaged, and we married six months after that. When you know, you know. Why waste time trying to talk yourself out of it?"

I've heard about how my grandparents met, started dating, and got married within a year. It always boggled my mind because I couldn't imagine making the decision to spend forever with any of the guys I dated in such a short time period. But, I'll admit that Simon is different. Not that I'm looking to get engaged anytime soon, but the idea doesn't give me hives either.

"Just please ixnay on the marriage talk when Simon is here," I said. "I don't want you scaring him off."

"I don't think you have to worry about scaring that boy off. He's not weak like the other ones you brought home."

"Granny Vi, I can't think of any reason you'd have to bring up marriage or engagement in a conversation with Simon."

I know my warning will go right over her head, but I have to say something and hope it sticks.

"I'll do my best not to bring those things up but it's hard to say where the conversation will flow."

I'm pretty sure she's being facetious, but with Granny Vi you never know. Shaking my head, I stood and walked over to the sink to rinse my mug. After setting it on the drying rack, I dried my hands, and turned back to face her.

"You seem to like Simon, so promise you'll go easy on him today."

She didn't even pretend to not know what I was talking about.

"With Simon there's not a lot to pick on, so he should be fine. I'll just be my usual

charming self."

That's about the best I can ask for with her. Now I have to talk to my parents and get them to make the same promise. But that will have to wait until after my nap.

SIMON

"Do I smell French toast?"

Shannon stepped behind me and looked over my shoulder.

"You do."

"I hope you're making some for me."

"Of course." I flipped six slices of French toast in quick succession. "There's sausage too. It's staying warm in the oven if you want to grab it. This is almost done."

She stepped away from me then came back holding the plate of sausage.

"Table or island?"

"Table."

I'm hoping to have a heart-to-heart with her and that's better done face-to-face.

I placed three slices of French toast on two plates, then carried them over to the table, where Shannon was sitting eating a piece of sausage.

"So what's the occasion?"

"For what?" I asked.

"French toast," she said, then shoved a forkful into her mouth.

I shrugged.

"I had a craving."

"Mmm, this is almost as good as dad's." She finished chewing then swallowed. "I'm surprised Keera didn't stay here last night."

"She had a long week and was exhausted. Plus she wanted to be home to help her grandmother with dinner. Speaking of, are you coming?"

"No, it's the first time you're hanging out with her family." She smirked and pointed at me with a sausage. "I don't want my awesomeness to overshadow you."

"You're so funny. Not."

"But in all seriousness, I really like Keera. You guys are cute together."

She and Zoe never really hit it off, and I can't blame my sister for that. Zoe took one look at Shannon and labeled her a *mean girl*. No matter what Shannon said or did, Zoe took it the wrong way. It made get-togethers less than pleasant.

"Thanks. Things are going well."

"That's great. You deserve it."

I couldn't have asked for a better lead-in to the conversation I want to have with Shannon. I'd planned on talking to her last night, but she was in bed when I got home.

"Is everything okay, Shan?"

She stabbed the last piece of French toast and dragged it through the puddle of syrup before popping it into her mouth. I continued eating. History has taught me that Shannon will answer when she's good and ready.

"No," she said, what seemed like an eternity later.

"What's wrong?"

"I don't know exactly." She shrugged. "I've been trying to figure it out, but keep coming up blank."

"What's happening?"

"I'm living this dream life in the city, but lately..." She trailed off, shaking her head. "I feel like I'm just going through the motions."

"Did something happen? Bad breakup?"

"Not really." She shrugged. "Not one big event anyway. I think it's just a bunch of little things piled together."

She picked up our dishes then walked over to the sink and washed them by hand. I got up, grabbed a towel, and dried, then put them into the cupboard. There are a lot of questions running through my head, but I kept them to myself. Now that I've broached the subject, Shannon will continue the conversation eventually. At least I hope she will.

We walked into the living room and settled onto opposite ends of the sectional sofa. Shannon picked up a throw pillow and hugged it to her chest. Neither of us said anything for a few minutes, but she finally spoke.

"You know that when I was offered that internship in Manhattan, I moved there and never looked back. I loved the city and every job I've had there. But now I just find it all exhausting and pointless."

She looked down at the pillow and traced the pattern with her index finger.

"I went to a counselor, thinking I might be depressed." She looked up at me and shrugged. "Other than not enjoying things I used to, I feel fine. But something is going on."

"What did he say?"

"*She* said she doesn't think I'm depressed. She thinks I'm just ready for a change. That just because working in the beauty industry in Manhattan was my dream at twenty, doesn't mean it'll be what I want to do for the rest of my life." Shannon shifted and stretched her legs out, crossing them at the ankles. "For six months, she had me keep a journal, detailing everything I did and how I felt before, during, and after each thing. That was really eye-opening because it was all there in black in white to read later. There was no mentally whitewashing my thoughts and feelings after the fact."

"So now that you know, what are you planning to do?"

She looked up at the ceiling and shook her head, then met my gaze again.

"I can't even believe I'm saying this, but I think I want to move back here."

That's the last thing I expected her to say.

"Really?"

"I know, I know. All I ever wanted to do was leave," she said. "But the past eighteen months or so, when I'm here, I feel like it's where I belong."

"Did you talk to Mom and Dad about this?"

"Not yet. I wanted to figure things out before saying anything to anyone. If you didn't ask me what's wrong, we wouldn't be talking about it now."

She stood and stretched, a sign that this conversation is over.

"I know this is a big decision for you, but for what it's worth, I'd be thrilled to have you back."

Leaning down, she gave me a hug.

"Thanks. I'll let you know when I have everything sorted out. I'm going to go shower then hit the road. Hopefully I'll miss the worst of the traffic."

CHAPTER 16

Keera

I just finished setting the table when the doorbell rang. My brother beat me to answering it and I gave him a warning look.

"Be nice."

"I'm always nice." He stuck his tongue out, then opened the door. "You must be Simon. I'm Keera's brother, Kevin."

With my brother's hulking body blocking the door, I couldn't see Simon. Kevin was being pleasant, basically making elevator conversation with my boyfriend while standing in the doorway. My sister-in-law Anna left for a business trip this morning, so unfortunately, she's not around to rein her husband in.

I was about to go over there when Granny Vi said, "Kevin move out of the way and let him come in."

Kevin stepped back and Simon walked through the door and smiled at me. He's wearing khakis and another of those untucked shirts, this one is solid burgundy.

I looked down at the bags in his hand.

"You didn't have to bring anything," I said.

"Of course I did." He leaned in and kissed my cheek then handed me one of the bags. "That one is for you. It's nothing big, but when I saw it, I thought of you."

"Those are the best gifts. Thank you."

I took the bag from him but before I checked its contents, I re-introduced him to my parents.

"You've met my parents, Ellen and Marty," I said. "And that's my brother Kevin."

"Yes, we met a few times at Party on the Patio," Simon said as he shook their hands.

"It's good to see you again," my mom said, then looked at me. "What's in the bag, Keera?"

I peeked inside then pulled out a big bag of cherry licorice nibs.

"You always used to keep them at your desk," Simon said.

"What'd you get?" Granny Vi asked.

"Licorice nibs."

"Very thoughtful." She looked at Simon. "For future reference, I prefer the black ones."

"Noted," he said, then held out the other bag to her. "These are for everyone, but you can do the honors."

Granny Vi peeked inside and smiled.

"Do I have to share?"

"That is entirely up to you."

She looked at me.

"I told you I like him."

At least she didn't call him "this one" like she tends to do.

"What'd he bring?" my mom asked.

"Caramel apples and peanut butter Smidgens from Gertrude Hawk."

My dad joined in the conversation.

"Oh, you're sharing those."

"Let's eat dinner before we start a war over dessert," I said.

"Life's short, eat dessert first," my mom said.

"Funny, that wasn't your motto when I was a kid."

"It definitely was, it just didn't apply to you," she said. "But you're an adult now, so I

guess it can."

"Nice. Another perk of adulthood."

Mom and Granny Vi went into the kitchen to put the finishing touches on dinner. I'd

helped earlier, but they both told me they have it under control now.

I took Simon's hand and we walked into the dining room followed by my dad and Kevin.

"Who was your favorite Party on the Patio band?" my dad asked Simon.

Most fathers ask about a guy's intentions or future plans, but being a musician, he

says he finds out all he needs to know by getting their music preferences. Anytime we went out somewhere that had a jukebox, his favorite thing to do was put a bunch of money in and have my boyfriend pick songs. Although to be fair, he also had Anna do it. He told Kevin to propose to her when she picked "Rosalita" by Bruce Springsteen, "Stone in Love" by Journey, and "American Woman" by The Guess Who.

"That's a tough one. They were all pretty good. The Jimmy Buffet one was fun, but I think that's because it had the whole Buffett party atmosphere. AC/DC and Journey were good too, but I think I liked the Fleetwood Mac band best. Was it Tusk?"

My dad smiled. Stevie Nicks is one of his all-time favorite singers. She's number one on his *freebie list*. So any fan of Stevie or Fleetwood Mac is a friend of his.

Mom and Granny Vi walked into the room carrying a platter and serving bowls. They set them down and sat.

"We're pretty informal here," Granny Vi said to Simon. "So feel free to just help yourself."

Even though that's the case, my past boyfriends usually sat back and waited for me to fill their plate. Simon dug right in and he complimented the food. Every time Brian ate with my family, instead of saying it was good, he'd talk about a healthier way to cook whatever we were eating. Sometimes he wouldn't eat at all. It was very annoying.

Another nice thing is that Simon is holding his own conversations with everyone at the table without me having to mediate. I've heard him discussing computers, his job, and his dad. Right now, he's telling my dad about his parents' trip.

"El, we should do that," he said.

"What size RV do you think we'd need to fit all the junk you'd want to bring?"

"My stuff is not junk."

My parents started bickering as they tend to do. I looked at Simon and rolled my eyes. His answering smile made my stomach flip. Which is a nice change from the knots it used to feel when my past boyfriends were around my family or friends. I don't know why I was so nervous about Simon meeting my family. He's so easygoing, I should have known he'd fit right in.

"When is it?" I heard Simon ask my dad.

"The Saturday after Thanksgiving at Finnegan's." My dad looked at me. "You're coming, right?"

"Definitely."

"Then why doesn't Simon know about it?"

"Because it's a month away and I've been focused on other things." I looked at Simon. "I hope you're available. It should be a good time."

"Yeah, I'll mention it to my parents too. They love that kind of music."

A couple weeks ago this conversation would have freaked me out, but I feel much more secure in my relationship now. Which is a good thing because it's looking like our families will be meeting next month.

SIMON

I JUST CHANGED INTO PAJAMA PANTS WHEN MY PHONE RANG.

"Hey, I didn't expect to hear from you tonight."

"Just making sure you're okay after meeting the family," Keera said.

"It was fun. You didn't need to be worried."

"Did I seem worried?"

Even though she couldn't see, I held up my hand with my thumb and index finger barely spaced apart.

"A little bit."

"Sorry, I have PTSD from the ghosts of boyfriends past."

"I get it. Zoe didn't like Shannon and it was always stressful."

"What was her problem? Shannon is awesome."

"So is your family."

"Yeah, they are." She sighed. "So what are you doing?"

"I just changed and was going to watch TV."

"Oh yeah? What are you wearing?"

That last question was asked in a low, sexy voice.

"Pajama pants."

"Anything else?"

"Nope."

"Hmm, I think I'd like to see that."

"I could send you a picture."

"As much as I'd like that, I think I'd rather see it in person."

I heard a noise in the background, then the doorbell rang.

"Is that you?"

"Hmm, could be."

I tossed my phone on the bed and ran downstairs. Sliding across the foyer, I slammed my palm against the door to stop. Unlocking it, I pulled it open and found the most beautiful girl in the world standing there.

"This is the best surprise ever."

Keera stepped over the threshold and I closed the door behind her. She placed her hands flat against my bare abdomen and slowly stroked up.

"We haven't been alone for a few days and I missed you, so I figured I'd come visit."

"I'm so glad you did."

She moved closer and pressed against me.

"I believe you said you were going to watch TV." I nodded. "Were you going to do that up in your room?" I nodded again and a sexy smile spread across Keera's face. "Why don't we head up there and...watch something?"

I grabbed her hand and practically dragged her up the stairs. By the time we reached my room, we were both laughing hysterically. She ran through the door and jumped into the middle of the bed. On her knees, she held her arms out to me. That's an invitation I definitely can't refuse.

Crawling onto the bed, I met her in the middle and pulled her against me, pressing our mouths together. The hungry kiss went on and on, and as our tongues teased and tasted, our hands stroked and explored.

Cupping her ass, I pressed Keera against my throbbing erection. She pulled her mouth from mine and sucked in a deep breath. Her hands moved up my chest to my shoulders and pushed. I hadn't been expecting that and fell back onto my elbows.

Keera shoved me the rest of the way down until I was lying flat on my back. Lifting her leg to straddle my thighs, she dragged her fingertips across my chest and down my stomach. Using just her index finger, she traced the edge of my pajamas.

"You know, when we worked together, I had no idea what a hot bod was hiding beneath those baggy clothes." She lowered her hands and stroked my erection, which was trying its best to burst through the fabric. "Especially this."

I'm not sure if I was supposed to say something to that, but since all the blood left my brain, I could barely think, much less speak. I was able to moan though, and that's exactly what I did when Keera leaned forward and pressed her pelvis against my erection. She kissed the center of my chest, then licked her way down and circled her tongue around my navel.

Backing away, she slipped her fingers into the edge of my waistband and slid them down. I felt cool air against my dick a second before Keera's hand wrapped around it.

"Keera, you're killing me."

Holding me tight, she moved her hand up and down in a

slow, seductive rhythm, dragging her thumb over the tip on each upstroke. I let out a low groan and Keera's eyes shifted to meet mine as she moved her hands to rest on my thighs.

"I think I should give you something to *really* groan about."

I held my breath as I watched her lean forward and run her tongue along the entire length of my cock. When she reached the top, Keera took just the tip into her mouth, then sucked and rolled her tongue around and around until I let out a long, low groan that seemed to come from the tips of my toes.

"*Shit.*" I curled my fingers into her hair. "Keera, that feels–"

I forgot whatever I was going to say when she lowered her mouth, taking me to the back of her throat, before pulling back and starting all over again. She settled into a rhythm designed to make me lose it, and it didn't take long before I felt my release tingling at the base of my spine.

Tightening my fingers against her scalp, I stopped her movements.

"Stop," I gasped. "Please stop."

She released me and I kept my eyes closed tight as I breathed in and out, trying to regain control. After a few seconds, I opened them.

"Sorry about that." Keera backed away as I shifted to sit. "It was almost over for a second there."

The corner of her mouth kicked up into a teasing smile.

"That wouldn't have been the worst thing."

I slid my pants down my legs and kicked them off the rest of the way. Moving to my knees, I shifted forward, urging Keera to lie back. When she did, I crawled between her thighs. Dipping my head, I nibbled along her collarbone and up her neck.

"I want to be inside you when I come," I whispered into her ear. Pulling back, I looked her in the eye. "Tell me what *you* want."

"I just want you."

Closing my eyes, I absorbed her words. Only in my wildest dreams did I ever think I'd have a chance with Keera. And here we are like this.

I shifted back and pulled a condom out of the bedside table. With record speed, I opened the foil packet, rolled the condom down my length, and settled between Keera's thighs. We both groaned as I thrust inside. I held still for several heartbeats, just enjoying the feel of her. But that didn't last long because Keera squeezed my dick from the inside as she wrapped her legs around my hips. I grit my teeth and prayed for stamina as I started to pump in and out, moving faster and faster as she met me thrust for thrust.

"Simon..."

Keera dug her fingers into my ass and tightened her thighs around my waist. Her inner muscles fluttered and I picked up the pace, giving us what we both needed. Soon they were squeezing my cock as Keera moaned her release. Seconds later, I let out my own long moan and collapsed on top of her.

CHAPTER 17

Keera

I RESTED MY HEAD AGAINST SIMON'S CHEST, ENJOYING THE slow, steady beat of his heart. This feeling of contentment is totally new to me, but I have to say I like it. I feel happy in a way I never have before.

Being with Simon is just *easy*. In the past, I would have equated that with boring. Growing up reading Nicholas Sparks novels and angsty young adult books must have brainwashed me into thinking relationships had to be full of drama to be real. But that's not the case. We always have fun, I love spending time with him, and the sex is off the charts.

"I can hear your mind spinning." He kissed the top of my head. "Hopefully they're good thoughts."

"They are." I kissed his chest. "I was thinking about how happy I am and how much I like being with you. How easy this is."

"I definitely like those thoughts. Makes me want to hear more."

Simon shifted onto his side and I did the same until we faced each other. The only light in the room is from the small lamp on the nightstand behind me, but it's bright enough so I could see his face.

"It makes me wish we got together sooner. Do you ever wonder why we never did?"

He reached out and tucked a loose strand of hair behind my ear then traced his finger along my jaw.

"You had boyfriends and then you were engaged. I was with Zoe and we moved in together. In the brief time we were both single..." He trailed off and shook his head.

When it didn't seem like he was going to continue, I shifted onto my elbow.

"What?"

"I wouldn't have asked you out because we were friends and we worked together. If you said no..." He shook his head again. "It would have been awkward and our friendship would have changed. I didn't want to lose that."

Didn't?

"It seems like you've put some thought into that."

"I've put way too much thought into that."

I nibbled at my bottom lip as I processed his words.

"So you thought about asking me out when we worked together?"

His mouth curled into an adorable smile.

"Only every minute of every day." My eyes widened. "You really had no idea?"

"No, I didn't." I shook my head and chuckled. "But Anjannette did."

"What makes you think that?"

"She always said you like me *that way*. Something about the way you looked at me."

"So what'd you say when she told you that?"

"I told her she was crazy." I shook my head. "I'm so glad I didn't know because it probably would have changed our friendship, especially when I was with Brian."

"That's exactly why I didn't say anything."

"So what made you ask me out?"

He took my hand in his and laced our fingers together.

"Indirectly it was Shannon."

"What did she do?"

"She kept setting me up with her friends. When I told her I didn't want to go on any more blind dates, she reminded me that I like to be in a relationship and I just needed to meet the right girl. I realized that I met the right girl, I just never asked her out."

"Me?"

"You."

"Oh wow."

I thought about all the times Simon and I spent together in the past. Even with hindsight, I don't see any glaring signs that he was into me.

"Is it really freaking you out?"

"Not really." He raised his brows. "It's not freaking me out, it's just making me question a few things."

"Like?"

"How would I have acted if I found out? What would I have said if you did ask me out? But mostly I'm wondering why I wasted my time with losers when you were right in front of me."

Simon wrapped his arm around my waist and pulled me closer until our noses practically touched.

"I don't want to waste time with what-ifs or could've-beens. I'm just happy that I finally asked you out, you said yes, and we're building on that."

I know I can't go back and change things, but I can't help

wondering where Simon and I would be if we got together back when we first met. If that had happened, I would have been saved a lot of aggravation and heartache for sure.

But maybe I needed to go through all that to become the person I am today so I could truly appreciate this. To truly appreciate him.

He gave me a soft kiss then pulled back to meet my gaze. As I got lost in his green depths, a warmth settled in my stomach, and a feeling I'm not ready to name made my heart flutter.

Shifting onto his back, Simon wrapped his arm around my shoulders and pulled me close until my cheek rested on his chest again. I closed my eyes and thanked the universe we finally got our timing right.

SIMON

"Dinner is late," Archer said. "It was supposed to be delivered seven minutes ago."

"Are you that hungry?" I asked.

"No, but they said it would be here by seven-thirty."

When the doorbell rang, I ran to it. If Archer answered, he'd lecture the poor delivery person about being late. It's happened before.

Andrew came downstairs freshly showered as I carried the Thai food into the kitchen.

"Oh good, the food is here. I'm starving."

Gaming is at his house tonight and since he had an emergency surgery, we're getting a late start. We settled around the table and dug into dinner.

"I know it's a while off, but are we doing a marathon Thanksgiving weekend?" Andrew asked after he'd put a good dent in his Drunken Noodles.

"I'll be at my aunt's in New Jersey until Friday night, but I'm available Saturday and Sunday."

Which is Archer's schedule every year.

"Keera's dad plays in a band and he just asked me to come to their fortieth anniversary show that Saturday night," I said. "But as far as I know, I'm available Saturday afternoon and Sunday."

"Maybe we can move it to another weekend." Andrew said, raising his voice at the end of the sentence turning it into a question.

We've been doing our gaming marathons Thanksgiving weekend since middle school. Despite trying to set them in stone, there've been a few times we've had to change the date. Archer usually isn't happy when that happens, but surprisingly, he's not complaining.

"The first Saturday in December is the recital at the pole studio, but other than that, I think I can be available."

We threw out some possible dates and agreed to check our calendars and make a decision by next week. Shannon can't believe we still do the marathons, but honestly, I don't see how it's any different than her girls' weekends.

"So can anyone go to that recital or is it invitation only?" Andrew asked.

"Anyone can go. Are you interested?"

"Sure."

I looked at Archer.

"I think I'll pass."

That doesn't surprise me at all.

"Do I get to meet Keera beforehand or is my first introduction to her going to be while she's spinning on a pole?" Andrew asked.

"No, I'll definitely set something up so you can meet."

"Things must be going well."

"Yeah, they are."

I don't want to jinx it, but things are actually great. In the past couple weeks, there's definitely been a shift between us. It's obvious our relationship has moved beyond the "enjoying each other's company" phase. While I've been half in love with Keera for a decade, that's definitely intensified since we've been spending time together. And it's obvious she feels something more too.

"Is she nicer than Zoe?" Archer asked.

The two of them never got along. Archer is one of my best friends, but he's kind of eccentric, and drove Zoe crazy.

"You'll like Keera."

"I hope so," he said. "I don't know how you tolerated Zoe all those years. Does Keera know you still talk to her?"

"I don't still talk to her."

"You helped with her computer a couple months ago."

"Yeah, but it's not like we chat every day. When we lived together, I set up her home office and she got a new computer so I helped her out and hooked it up."

Zoe and I didn't have a bad breakup, our relationship just kind of fizzled out. I've seen and spoken to her a handful of times since we split and it's always friendly. There's really no reason for it not to be.

"And you had lunch," he pointed out.

"She bought me lunch as a thank you."

"Just make sure you don't end up in a love triangle."

"Zoe and I broke up years ago so I don't think there's any chance of that," I said. "Besides, I'm not interested in anyone but Keera."

CHAPTER 18

Keera

I LOOKED AROUND DR. GREEN'S RECEPTION AREA, THINKING about the first time I sat here. It was just last year yet it seems like forever ago. I'd just been let go from Wilder and I was hooking up with one loser after another in an attempt to get over a toxic relationship. It was definitely a low point in my life.

"Keera?" I looked up at the sound of Dr. Green's voice. "Come on in."

I followed her into her office and settled in my usual comfy leather chair. She picked up a notebook and pen from her desk and sat across from me.

"So, it's been about six weeks since you've been here. How's it been going?"

"Pretty well, actually."

"What's been happening?"

"The studio is thriving. We held a very successful open house a few weeks ago and classes have been packed. Plus we're starting a beginner's series this Saturday. So work is going well."

"That's good to hear. You were so worried when you got laid off. But the studio seems to be working out and it suits you much better."

"I definitely enjoy it more, and I feel like I'm actually making a difference. Pole dance helped me so much with body image and it's how I met some of my best friends. I love welcoming people into the community and watching them thrive and grow."

I stopped talking and waited until she finished taking notes before filling her in on the rest of the changes in my life.

"And I started dating someone."

"Oh?"

I'm amazed at her poker face. If I was a counselor and had heard the bad and the ugly of my dating life, I'm not sure my expression would be so neutral at that announcement.

"We've only been seeing each other a few weeks, but we used to work together so I've known him for about ten years."

"Did you ever date before?"

"No, I never thought of him like that."

"But that's obviously changed."

"Yeah."

"So how'd you end up going out?"

"He came to the open house and asked me out. My first instinct was to turn him down. But I didn't. Instead, I told him I'd let him know."

"So what made you say yes?"

"Anjannette convinced me to give him a chance. She's

said for years that Simon had the hots for me. I thought she was crazy, but it turns out she was right."

I told her about the conversation Simon and I had the other night.

"So when did your feelings toward him change?"

"During that first date," I said. "At first it was strange. I kept thinking 'this is Simon' but once I got out of my head, I opened up to the possibility of something more between us. And when he kissed me..." I trailed off and thought about that first kiss.

"You don't have to say any more about that. Your smile speaks volumes," she said. "So tell me about Simon."

"He's so sweet and really smart, and he treats me well. Definitely not my usual type, which Anjannette reminded me is a good thing." We both chuckled at that. "At first I was worried I'd do something to mess things up, but so far, so good."

"Why did you think that?"

"You know about my past relationships. My track record isn't great."

"But things are different with Simon."

Her words were more a statement than a question, but I answered anyway.

"They definitely are, but all the old baggage is still there. For instance, I was a nervous wreck when my grandmother invited Simon to Sunday dinner with my family."

"It's pretty normal to be nervous for something like that."

"Yeah, but what I felt went beyond what's normal and it definitely stems from past experiences. Every time Brian and I spent any time with my family, we usually ended up fighting. Or I ended up stroking his ego for a week. Sometimes both. And Jason was the same before him. I projected that onto Simon and expected him to react the same way."

"But it went okay?"

"It went great, but there's no reason it wouldn't have. Simon isn't like Brian or Jason, or any of the other guys. Logically I know that, but I've spent a lot of time with idiots and none with good guys like him. I just don't want to ruin things because of a knee-jerk reaction."

"If he's as good as you say, he'll understand," she said. "From what it sounds like, you're in a healthy relationship for the first time. Just go with the flow and enjoy it. Trust yourself, but more importantly, trust Simon."

SIMON

KEERA AND I JUST FINISHED EATING WHEN GRANNY VI CAME breezing through the front door, her arms full of packages.

"Do you need help?" I asked.

"No, I'm good." She plopped the bags down on the counter. "I'm heading to New York tomorrow with my friends. These are some snacks."

She reached into one bag and pulled out Snickers bars, Pringles, and M&M's.

"Looks like it's going to be a fun trip," I said.

"Road trip snacks should always look like a toddler picked them."

"Just make sure you don't overdo it," Keera said. "You don't want your sugar going

bonkers again."

"Oh psshhh. I'll be fine."

"You're staying with Darren and Cole, right?"

"Yes, their new apartment has four bedrooms." She looked at me. "Darren is my friend June's son and Cole is his husband. They usually come here to visit, but once or twice a year, they bring her to the city and invite Irene and me along. I don't know exactly what they do for a living, but they're loaded." She dragged out that last word.

"That definitely makes living in the city more enjoyable."

"Where does Shannon live?" Keera asked.

"Upper East Side."

For now. But I didn't say that. Shannon hasn't told our parents yet, and they should know before anyone else.

"I have no idea where Darren and Cole live," Granny Vi said. "I just go wherever the limo takes me."

"A limo?" I whistled. "Nice touch."

"They treat us well."

"You deserve it."

She looked at Keera.

"Hold on to this one."

"Granny Vi," Keera sighed.

"I'm sorry. Hold on to *Simon*." She hugged Keera from behind then straightened. "I'm going to finish packing and go to sleep. You kids can Netflix and chill or whatever it is you do. I won't be back downstairs tonight."

"Good night," I said.

She winked then headed up the stairs.

Keera stood and I helped her clear the table.

"What was that about?" I asked as we tossed everything into the garbage.

"What?"

"*Hold on to Simon.*"

"I hate it when she refers to you as 'this one.' It just sounds bad."

"I'm sure she doesn't mean anything by it." Keera looked at me and blinked. "What?"

"Nothing." She wrapped her arms around my waist and rested her head against my chest. "But I think I'll listen to Granny Vi and hold on to you."

"That sounds good to me." I kissed the top of her head. "Are we gonna Netflix and chill like she said?"

Keera straightened to look me in the eye.

"Isn't she incorrigible?"

"She's actually pretty awesome."

"I think so too, even though she drives me crazy sometimes." I followed her into the living room and we settled onto the couch. She picked up the remote and turned on the TV. "What do you feel like watching?"

"Anything is fine."

"There's an *It's Always Sunny in Philadelphia* marathon on."

"That's perfect."

She changed the channel, set down the remote, and settled against me.

"The next few weeks are going to be crazy."

"If there's anything I can do to make things easier for you, just let me know."

"Do you want to take over some of the private lessons I have set up?"

"Sure. Just text me the moves."

She chuckled at that and tightened her hold on my waist.

"But seriously, I appreciate it. You're always so supportive."

From conversations we've had in the past, I know Brian

hated the fact that Keera loved pole so much. Knowing what I do about their relationship, I'm guessing it wasn't the pole dance he objected to so much as the friends she found in that community.

We settled in to watch TV and just quietly enjoy each other's company. I swear I could do this for the rest of my life and be a happy man.

CHAPTER 19

Keera

"I can't believe this is here," Anjannette said. "When we first started planning the beginner class, it seemed so far away."

"Time flies when you're having fun."

"It also flies when you're busy as hell."

"I guess that means the next few weeks are going to fly. Between regular classes, this beginner series, and getting ready for the recital, we should probably just bring in mattresses and sleep here."

"It's going to be crazy for sure."

I heard the front door open and voices out in the hallway.

"Sounds like some of our students are here. Do you want to greet or check in?"

"I'll greet. It'll help me burn some of my nervous energy."

"Remember, it's just another class."

"It's something new and you know I like to freak out over things I've never done before."

Before I could respond, three women walked through the door.

I woke up the computer and opened the booking program. We have twenty students registered, which is the max we wanted in the class. Since we have ten poles, we'll have two groups. As this is our first time doing this type of class, we don't know what to expect as far as dropouts. I guess we'll find out.

After checking in those first three women, there was a little gap, and then a bunch of people arrived at once and a small line formed.

"Hi," I said to the next person. "What's your name?"

"Sacha Mullins."

I found her registration and read the comments.

"You signed up for two people. Did you find someone to come with you?"

"I did."

"Great! I just need a name and are they here yet?"

"Yes, she is."

She moved slightly to the side and the woman who'd been standing just behind her stepped forward.

"The name is Zoe Fields."

I looked up and saw Simon's ex standing right in front of me.

"Oh uh, hi Zoe."

We've been in each other's company enough that I couldn't pretend to not know her.

"I thought that was you Keera," she said. "It's funny, when Sacha asked me if I wanted to do this, I mentioned you because I remember you took classes. I thought you went to a different studio though."

"Yeah, I used to, but when Anjannette opened this studio I moved. Now I work here and I'm a partner."

"Did you leave Wilder?"

"They laid me off last year."

"I'm sorry to hear that."

"Thanks. It worked out for the best though. I'm here doing what I love." Wanting to end this conversation, I said, "You're all checked in under your name."

"Great." She started to leave then turned back around. "I'm surprised Simon didn't mention you weren't working with him anymore."

I frowned.

"When would he have mentioned it?"

"I got a new computer a couple months ago and he came over to hook it up to the system he put together in my home office, then we had lunch and got caught up."

A couple women stepped behind Zoe and we ended the conversation there so I could take care of them. I did my best to hide my shock at what she just told me as I checked the final students in.

I had no idea she and Simon were still in touch. As far as I knew, they broke up and that was it. In my experience, hanging out with an ex just causes trouble. Before I could mentally spiral out of control thinking about it, Anjannette signaled that it was time to start. I stood and walked over to the front of the room.

"Thank you for being here, everyone," Anjannette said. "This is our inaugural beginner series. Which basically means that you're our Guinea pigs."

Everyone laughed at that, even though it's partially true.

"This is an eight-week series that builds upon itself week after week, so try not to miss a class. We emailed a schedule but I want to take a second to go over it. We're here every

Saturday from ten to noon except Thanksgiving weekend. The last class is the Saturday before Christmas." She looked at me. "Anything you want to add?"

What I want to do is call Simon and ask him why the fuck he's hanging out with his ex-girlfriend. But instead, I put on my happy face and said something inspiring.

"I just want to warn you that this is hard. Anjannette floats up that pole and makes it look easy, but it's not. And sometimes it hurts. Hell, *most* times it hurts. But it's so worth it. So even if we show you something and you don't get it the first time, just keep on trying. Eventually you'll get it and you'll be stronger in the process."

"Okay," Anjannette said. "Now that Keera has scared the hell out of you, let's get warmed up."

Simon

Keera came outside as soon as I pulled up to the curb. I usually walk up to the door when I pick her up, so I was surprised to see her heading toward me. Scrambling out of the car, I ran around the front and opened the door, giving her a quick kiss before she settled into the passenger seat.

I got behind the wheel and smiled over at her.

"I can't wait to hear about the beginner class." I started the car. "How did it go?"

"It went well."

Her flat tone had me concerned. In fact, something has seemed off with her all day.

She answered my call with a text and my texts with one-word answers. That's definitely not normal for Keera.

"You okay?"

She shrugged. I don't have a whole lot of experience with women, but I know enough about them to realize a shrug with no words is never good.

"Did the class not go well?"

"No, it was good."

"Then what's wrong?"

She was looking out her window and I didn't think she was going to answer, but after

several minutes, she spoke.

"Zoe is in the class."

"Okay?"

Out of the corner of my eye, I saw Keera turn her head to look at me. I glanced at her for a second before shifting my eyes back to the road.

"I was surprised when she told me the two of you still talk."

This is the second time this has been brought up, first by Archer and now Keera, and I have no idea why it's an issue.

"I haven't talked to her for a few months."

"But you did, and you got together for lunch."

"She bought me lunch because I hooked up her new computer to the system I set up for her a few years ago."

I turned into the parking lot and pulled into a spot. We're meeting Keera's friends at Poor Richard's, and Andrew and Archer are coming, too. I was psyched about everyone meeting, but right now I'm not so sure. If Keera is really upset about Zoe, it could be a stressful night.

"Is that something you do often?"

"Set up her computer? No."

She looked at me like I'm the biggest moron in the world.

"Get together with her. Talk to her."

"No."

"Then how did you end up fixing her computer?"

"She called and asked me."

"And you just did it?"

"Why wouldn't I?"

"Because you broke up."

Once she said that, I realized the issue. I don't know if Keera has ever had an amicable breakup. I'm not sure what happened with her and Jason, but I know it wasn't good. And Brian cheated on her and it was a whole shitshow.

"We didn't have a bad breakup." I shifted to better face her. "Keera, trust me when I tell you that there's nothing between Zoe and me. Our relationship was over years ago. That being said, we're still on friendly terms. When she asked me how to hook up her new computer, I said I could do it. And that was at least a month before you and I started dating."

She looked down at her lap and took in a deep breath then met my gaze again.

"When I saw Zoe in class, it threw me for a loop. But when she told me you hooked up her computer and had lunch, I went off the deep end imagining all kinds of things."

"Stop imagining. I'm with you and it's right where I want to be."

"Thank you," she said.

"For what?"

"Being sweet and not making me feel crazy even when I act like I am."

"You're very welcome." I leaned in and gave her a quick kiss. "Come on, let's go introduce our friends."

We walked into Poor Richard's and Andrew, Archer,

Anjannette, and Leo were already there. They were even sitting at the same table.

"How did you know each other?" I asked when they told me there was no need for introductions.

"I recognized Leo," Archer said.

Even though he's not athletically inclined, Archer is basically a sports savant. He loves watching most sports and he has stats memorized for them all. He also studies the physics of the games because he finds it fascinating. That's a quote from him.

Eve and Sophie joined us and a few minutes later a couple I never met showed up.

"Simon, Andrew, Archer, this is Rosa Wright and her husband Mason. Rosa is one of our favorite students."

We shook hands then settled in around the table again. Soon it was filled with food and drink and everyone was having a great time, even Archer.

I kept a close eye on Keera, who was acting more like her usual self. Thankfully there was no sign of her earlier upset. Hopefully I reassured her that she has nothing to worry about. I'm a one-woman man and she's most definitely the one woman for me.

CHAPTER 20

Keera

I sat against the wall and watched Sophie and Eve go through their routine. What there is of it anyway.

They're doing a doubles routine to "Unwritten" by Natasha Bedingfield in this year's recital. The song is appropriate on a couple levels for the women. First, they're both authors and second, they've both recently divorced and are basically starting their lives over.

"So what do you think?" Sophie asked. "What can we add?"

"I like what you have so far. You've done a great job figuring out things you can do together on the same pole. Now you can add things you can do on your own pole. For instance, where she sings 'release your inhibitions, feel the rain on your skin' later in the song, I think it would be really cool if you added synchronized drops."

They looked at each other then both nodded at me. Since they like that, I continued.

"If you want to work on spin pole, you could add some cool spins. Maybe three or four flowing into the other. Just off the top of my head, start off with a skating spin, then climb to the top and do a genie, then a cupid, and a fireman's spin down to the floor."

We listened to the song a couple times and I tried to picture some choreography in my head. I don't want to totally change what they've done so we just worked on adding to it. Putting them on separate poles made that a lot easier.

When Anjannette walked through the door, I realized our hour was almost up.

"Why don't you do a drop to see how in sync you can be?"

Anjannette sat next to me and we watched them climb the pole, settle into a pole sit, curl into a ball, and drop.

"Not bad," I said. "You weren't totally in sync, but since this recital is just for fun, it'll work. Now try the spin combo we discussed."

As I expected, the spins need some work. Sophie is spinning faster than Eve and it's throwing off the rhythm. They reached the floor within a second of each other, so that's something.

"You guys look good," I said. "We just need to tweak a couple things, add some floor work, and you'll be good."

"Can we do that in six weeks?" Eve asked.

"Five weeks because we're off for Thanksgiving." Sophie added.

"You'll be fine." I stood and stretched out my legs. "The hard part is figuring out what to do. After that, it just takes practice." I looked at Sophie. "You did this last year so you know the drill. Tell Eve to trust the process."

"I've never been in a dance recital in my life," Eve said. "I don't know how I let you talk me into this," she said to Sophie. Then she looked at Anjannette and me. "Or how I let the two of you talk me into being in the intermediate class dance."

"It'll be fun," Anjannette said. "You'll see."

"Who else is in the class dance besides us?" Sophie asked.

"Chelsea, Paisley, Tasha, Tabitha, and Phoebe. And of course, Keera." Anjannette looked

at the clock. "Everyone should be here in a half hour or so."

"I'm going to hit the bathroom," Eve said and Sophie joined her as she left the studio to hit the ladies' room across the hall.

We've scheduled the practices with enough of a gap between so if one group runs late it doesn't screw up the whole schedule. Plus it gives people participating in multiple dances a chance to rest in between.

I walked over to the desk and grabbed my purse, hoping to find a granola bar or something to eat but came up empty.

"Do you have anything to eat?" I asked Anjannette. "I'm starving."

"No, sorry," she said.

"Do you think I have time to run to the store and grab something?"

"Go. I can handle things for a few minutes if you're not back. You need to eat so you don't faint."

"Yeah, I wouldn't want to break one of your class rules."

I slipped on my shoes, picked up my purse, and headed out the door. Before I got to the exit, the big door opened and a man walked in carrying five trays of pizza. The foyer filled with smells of cheesy, tomato-y, and garlicky goodness and my mouth watered.

It took all my willpower not to grab a tray and run. After all, the owner wouldn't be able to chase me without dropping the other pizza. That thought had just left my head when the man carrying the precious cargo peeked his head around the stack.

"Simon?"

Simon

"Let me help you," Keera said.

She loosened my load by taking the top two trays off the stack.

"I know you're going to be here until at least eleven so I figured I'd bring you ladies something to eat."

"You are a godsend. I'm starving and was just running to the corner store to grab something." She took in a deep breath and moaned. "Is this Vince's pizza?"

"It is."

"My favorite."

I followed her into the studio and set the boxes down on the desk next to hers.

"Simon, you win the best boyfriend of the day prize," Anjannette said. "Thank you."

"You're welcome."

Keera pulled paper plates and napkins out of the drawer and set them on top of the desk.

Anjannette grabbed three bottles of water from the mini-fridge.

"Oh no, this is for you," I said. "I didn't plan on staying."

"You have to at least have a slice," Keera said. "Unless you have somewhere to be."

"Nope, I'm just going home."

She handed me a plate with two slices.

"Then please stay."

How can I refuse an invitation like that?

"Do I smell pizza?" Sophie asked as she and Eve walked through the door.

"You do," Keera said. "Simon brought us sustenance."

They looked at me.

"Seriously?" Eve asked.

I nodded as I chewed the big bite I'd just taken. I've already eaten dinner, but Vince's is

my favorite pizza too and I can't resist.

"Thank you," they said in unison.

I'd just finished eating when three women entered the studio. Keera introduced Chelsea, Tabitha, and I already met Phoebe at the axe throwing place. They just helped themselves to pizza when Paisley and Tasha arrived and joined in. It's nice putting faces to some of the names Keera has mentioned.

By the time everyone was done eating, four and a half of the five trays were gone.

"I better let you ladies get to it," I said. "I'll take the empty boxes with me."

"We can throw them in the dumpster," Keera said. "Here, I'll help you."

Once again, she took the top two boxes off the stack I was holding. I followed her out the door. We walked to the end of the parking lot and she tossed her boxes into the dumpster tucked way in the back corner and I did the same.

Keera took my hand in hers and squeezed as we walked back to the front of the building.

"Thank you so much for bringing that. It was so thoughtful."

"From our years working together, I know you don't usually pack meals. So you wouldn't have been eating until almost midnight."

"And you brought enough for everyone."

"I couldn't remember all the names of who was going to be here, but I figured if I

brought enough for ten, I'd be good."

She moved closer and wrapped her arms around my waist and rested her head against my chest.

"You're perfect, you know that?"

I figured that was a rhetorical question, so I didn't answer. She shifted back and looked me in the eye.

"Could I stay with you tonight?"

"Sure."

"I probably won't get there until close to midnight."

"That's fine."

"And I may be too tired to do much more than sleep."

I kissed her forehead.

"You're always welcome in my bed."

The corner of her mouth kicked up into an adorable smile.

"Cool." She leaned forward and kissed me. "I'll see you later."

CHAPTER 21

Keera

"I can't believe how gorgeous the weather is today," I said.

"It's definitely a perfect day for a bike ride."

The warm breeze blew through the car window and my hair floated around my head making me look like Medusa. I grabbed a scrunchie from my purse and pulled it into a messy bun.

"I just hope I don't kill myself."

"You'll be fine," Simon said, then looked at me and smiled. "It's like riding a bike."

"Ha ha, you're so funny."

Simon is surprisingly outdoorsy and today we're going bike riding on the Heritage Trail. I'm borrowing Shannon's bike because I don't have one of my own. My parents got rid of the one I rode when I was younger years ago.

I've had an exhausting week and it's nice having today

off. Last year, Anjannette and I worked seven days a week leading up to the recital but we decided to keep our Sundays off this year. We'll reevaluate as we get closer to the date, but I'm confident everyone's dances will get perfected without burning ourselves out.

"You can change that," Simon said.

I hadn't been paying attention to the radio, but once he said that, I heard a football game being broadcast on whatever station he had on.

Habit had me pressing 6, which is where Rock 107 is on my presets. That brought up Magic 93, which is number 2 in my car. My presets are in numerical order and I wondered how Simon set up his so I started pressing buttons.

After going through the stations a couple times, I couldn't find a rhyme or reason to the order. So I asked.

"What do you mean, how are they set up?"

"I do mine in numerical order, low to high."

"I don't have them in any specific order."

"What do you mean you don't have them in any order?"

"I think my words were pretty clear."

"So you're telling me that your presets just have random stations on them?"

"That's what I'm saying."

"Like some kind of sociopath?"

Simon looked at me, brow raised.

"Sociopath?"

I nodded.

"I'm not sure I feel safe riding a bike on a deserted trail with you."

"There is something seriously wrong with you," he said with a chuckle.

"Me? I'm not the one saving stations randomly in my presets."

He turned into the parking lot next to the trail and pulled into a spot. After shifting the car into park, he turned to face me.

"Why don't you set my channels for me?"

"Really?"

"Please."

He gestured toward the radio.

I released my seatbelt and shifted forward and got to work. It only took me a minute to have his presets organized in numerical order, like mine.

"There," I said. "All set."

"Feel better?"

"Much."

We got out of the car and Simon removed the bikes from the rack. He opened the back passenger door and retrieved two helmets and handed one to me. I don't like wearing hats of any kind, but this one is a necessary evil.

I took the scrunchie out of my hair and slipped it onto my wrist.

"This isn't going to be pretty."

I tucked my hair behind my ears and put the helmet on then snapped the chinstrap into place.

"You look adorable, as always."

I almost blurted out "Love is blind," but thankfully caught myself.

"And you are too kind," I said instead.

"Not kind, just truthful." He gave me a quick kiss then stepped back to put on his helmet. "Ready to hit the trail?"

"As I'll ever be."

I grabbed the handlebars, then carefully mounted the bike and put my right foot on the

pedal. It's been a long time since I've done this, but after getting off to a wobbly start, I found my balance.

As I slowly moved along the trail, Simon stayed by my side, matching my pace which I appreciate. Brian never wanted to do anything like this with me because he said I was too slow. Even if we just went shopping, he was five feet in front of me. At first, I rushed to keep up, but after a few years just kept to my own pace.

"I've never been on this trail. It's pretty," I said, shaking my ex from my thoughts.

"It's a great place to ride a bike. I hate riding on the street because drivers don't respect the bike lanes, if there even is one. And the trails at the state parks are a little more intense. It's nice to just come here and ride without working too hard."

"I'm all about not working too hard."

"You pole dance. That's not exactly easy."

"It's not." I shrugged. "But it's funny, I never think of it as exercise. Not like hiking, biking, or jogging anyway."

Simon pulled in front of me so the family of four coming toward us could easily get by. Once they passed, he slowed down so we were side-by-side again.

"Speaking of pole dance," he said. "I never asked what Zoe said when you told her we're dating."

Simon

Keera glanced over at me and I knew the answer to my question without her saying a word. She hit a small bump and jerked her head to look straight ahead and gained control of her bike.

I spotted a bench in the near distance and nudged my head in its direction.

"Let's take a break."

Pulling over to the side, I got off my bike and held Keera's handlebars as she got off hers. She walked around and shook out her legs, then stretched forward and touched her toes. I was enjoying the view and felt a little bummed when she straightened to look at me.

"I'm glad we stopped. I didn't realize my butt was numb."

She wiggled her ass and I couldn't resist touching her for another second. I walked over and pulled her into my arms. Our helmets bumped as I pressed my lips to hers. I tilted my head and opened my mouth wider, deepening the kiss as I pulled her against me. Moving my hands down her back, I cupped her ass and squeezed. Keera's moan vibrated against my chest and her leg wrapped around my calf as she pressed closer.

I slowed things down when I heard voices. Thankfully they were far enough off and I had enough time to slowly end the kiss. I curled my hand around hers and we walked over to the bench and sat.

She removed her helmet and dragged her fingers through her thick, brown hair and I itched to do the same. Instead, I rested my arm against the back of the bench. We sat in silence for a few minutes as the voices we'd heard got louder. Soon the people approached, then waved as they walked by. Once they were out of sight, I shifted toward Keera.

"So based on the look on your face earlier, I'm guessing you didn't tell Zoe we're dating."

"No, I didn't."

"Any reason why?"

"I was so shocked to see her and then we had class." She seemed to think for a second. "I guess I could have said something after class, but it would have seemed so random to approach her and just bring it up."

I guess she has a point. But I need to make sure things are clear between us.

"But you're not opposed to letting her know? Or letting anyone know?"

She looked confused by my questions, but slowly shook her head.

"My family and close friends all know we're dating. As far as Zoe goes, I think you'd be the one who'd be more concerned about her knowing or not knowing."

"I want *everyone* to know. We really haven't talked about it, but I guess now's as good a time as any." I placed my hand over hers and squeezed. "I'm not dating anyone else and don't want to."

The corner of her mouth curled up into an adorable smile.

"Simon Parker, are you asking me to go steady?"

"I am."

"Yes."

She mouthed the word more than said it and I moved closer, turning my head slightly toward her.

"Sorry, I didn't quite hear that."

Placing her hand on my shoulder, Keera shifted forward until her mouth brushed against my ear.

"Yes."

Her warm breath caressed my skin and goosebumps broke out all over my body.

I turned my head and brushed the tip of my nose against hers before placing a soft kiss on her lips. Pulling back, I tucked a stray hair behind her ear.

"Now that that's settled, why don't we head back and grab some lunch?'

"Sounds perfect."

CHAPTER 22

Keera

"Thanks so much, Anjannette. I really appreciate it."

"There's nothing to thank me for. You held down the fort while I was traveling during baseball season," she said. "Just pop some Midol, eat a bunch of chocolate, and relax."

"Right now I just want to curl into a ball and sleep. But I'm sure chocolate is in my near future," I said. "I should be okay tomorrow, but if not, I'll let you know."

"No worries. I have it all under control. Talk to you later."

I hung up then turned onto my side, pressed the pillow against my stomach, and let out a loud groan.

"Everything okay in there?"

"No, I think I'm dying."

Granny Vi walked into the living room and looked at me curled up on the couch.

"It's just your period. I think you'll survive."

"Have a little compassion. It feels like my uterus is tied

into a knot, my boobs are killing me, and my lower back and thighs are achy." I tightened my hold on the pillow. "*And* it feels like there's an ice pick jabbing up my hoo-ha."

She settled into her recliner and turned on the TV.

"I thought your birth control pills took care of those issues."

"They usually do. It's been a long time since I had cramps like this and I forgot how much it sucks."

"What do you think is going on?"

"I have no idea, but if it happens again next month, I'll have to call my gynecologist."

"Do you want something to eat or drink?"

"No thanks. I have tea and I'm not hungry. I'm just gonna take a nap and hope it goes away while I sleep."

"How about a *Gilmore Girls* marathon to fall asleep to? That always makes you feel better."

"I'll never say no to Luke and Lorelai." I picked up my phone. "But first I have to call Simon and cancel our date tonight."

She switched on Netflix to bring up the show while I dialed Simon.

"Hey Keera."

"Hi."

"What's wrong?"

What a guy. I could have been bleeding out of my eyeballs and Brian wouldn't have realized something was wrong. Simon knows after hearing one word over the phone.

"I have to cancel tonight. I'm not feeling well."

"Oh no, what's wrong?"

"I–"

I hesitated for a second for whatever reason. I'm sure Simon can handle hearing about my period issues.

"I'm exhausted and am having really bad cramps."

"Is there anything I can do to help?"

"I appreciate the offer, but no. I'm going to take a nap, maybe watch TV.

Anjannette is covering my class and lessons tonight."

"You must really feel bad if you're not going to the studio."

"Yeah, it sucks. I used to have issues like this when I was younger, but after I started taking birth control, the worst of it went away. So I don't know what's going on."

"Shannon had similar problems when we were in high school and I remember how miserable it was for her." He chuckled. "I also remember the *discussion* about whether or not she should go on birth control. My dad was afraid it would, and I quote, 'give her permission' to have sex."

Anna once told me that in her experience, guys with sisters make better boyfriends. Maybe she's onto something.

"There was a similar *discussion* between my parents, although my dad wouldn't give a specific reason, he'd just say 'because.'"

"See, we have more in common than we originally thought."

"I guess we do."

"I'll let you go so you can take that nap," he said, then added, "And I really am sorry you have to deal with this."

"Thanks. I'll talk to you later."

I hung up the phone and tucked it under my pillow.

"Should I start the show or do you just want to lay there with that sappy smile on your face?"

I picked up my head, looked over at her, and smiled.

"Start the show. I can multitask."

SIMON

I PICKED UP A QUART OF CHICKEN NOODLE SOUP, WING BITES, A cheeseburger, and fries with gravy from Joyce's. Then I stopped at the bakery and grabbed an assortment of cupcakes and headed to Keera's. She sounded so miserable on the phone, I figured I'd drop off some comfort food.

I parked in the driveway, grabbed the bag and box from the passenger seat, and got out of the car. The front door opened and Granny Vi walked out of the house as I stepped onto the porch.

"Oh hi, Simon," she said.

"Hi." I held up the items in my hand. "I brought some food for Keera."

"That's so sweet of you." She opened the door wider. "Go on in. She's curled up on the couch."

"I don't want to wake her. I know she's not feeling well."

"I'm awake," Keera yelled from inside.

"I'm heading out to dinner with a couple friends so you kids can relax and hang out without an old lady hanging around." A car pulled up to the curb and Granny Vi waved. "Perfect timing. Have fun."

"You too."

I watched as she walked down the steps, then the side-walk, and got into the car. She

waved as they pulled away and I turned and walked into the house. Keera was curled up on the couch, wrapped in a pink quilt with only her head visible.

"This is a nice surprise," she said.

"I just wanted to drop off some dinner." I placed the bags on the coffee table. "Are you hungry?"

"What'd you bring?"

I pulled each container out of the bag, detailing the contents of each.

"Mmm, my mouth is watering over here." She pushed up onto her elbow then shifted against the arm of the couch. "Which is funny because I just told Granny Vi I wasn't hungry."

"You didn't see the best part."

I opened the bakery box, showing her its contents.

"Are those red velvet?"

"Yep. I got the last two. There's also a chocolate with salted caramel icing, white with mocha icing, chocolate chip with white icing, and chocolate with chocolate fudge icing."

"You are a prince among men, Simon Parker." She patted the couch next to her. "Sit and help me eat this feast."

"I didn't plan on staying. I know you're not feeling well."

"Please stay. You always make me feel better."

How could I say no to that?

"Okay." I leaned down and kissed her forehead. "Do you need a drink?"

She picked up her tumbler and shook it.

"Yeah, I guess I do," she said and shifted to stand.

"No, I got it. Just tell me what you want."

"What I really, really want?"

"You must be feeling at least a little better if you're quoting the Spice Girls." I took the tumbler from her. "Water?"

"That sounds good. There's a filter on the sink."

"Ice?"

"Yes."

I went to the kitchen and filled her tumbler and a glass of water for myself.

"Need anything else from in here?"

"Nope, just you."

When I walked back into the living room, Keera was sitting cross-legged eating fries with gravy.

"Thank you for bringing this. Nothing like fat and sugar to cure what ails you."

I sat on the couch, shifting to face her.

"And *Gilmore Girls*."

"Definitely. Being transported to Stars Hollow always takes my mind off my issues."

"I think Shannon has watched this series all the way through at least ten times."

"Same."

She popped a fry into her mouth then held out the container to me. I shook my head.

"I got this for you."

"You can't expect me to eat all of this. A Joyce's burger alone could feed a family of four."

"You can always finish it later or tomorrow."

"Did you eat yet?"

"No, I have leftovers at home."

She leaned forward and grabbed the wing bites container then handed it to me with the top popped open.

"Eat."

"Yes, ma'am."

I reached into the bag and pulled out a plastic fork, then stabbed a piece of chicken and shoved it into my mouth. I speared another and held it out to her. She took it and smiled at me as she chewed.

"I'm really happy you came over tonight."

"Me too."

We watched TV and finished most of the food.

"I'm so stuffed," Keera said, as she shifted next to me.

I wrapped my arm around her shoulders and she rested her head against my chest as another episode of Gilmore

Girls started. This has never been my favorite show, but watching it like this with Keera makes it much more palatable.

"This is my absolute favorite episode."

"Why's that?"

"It's the one where Luke and Lorelai kiss for the first time."

She wrapped her arm around my waist and snuggled closer.

As the show went on, I mentally chuckled at the parallels between Luke and me. He'd been secretly in love with Lorelai, but for years they remained just friends and dated the wrong people. And like Luke, I finally grew a set and asked Keera out. However, I don't plan on screwing things up the way the fictional couple did.

The show ended and Keera pulled back to look at me. Her eyes shimmered with tears and I reached up to wipe one that had escaped from her cheek.

"Why are you crying?"

"Fucking hormones," she mumbled as she swiped at her eyes. "I've watched this episode a million times and never cried but now..."

"Now what?" I asked when she didn't seem inclined to finish her sentence.

"Between my hormones and this thing between us, I'm all sappy."

"'This thing between us?'"

"It's definitely a good thing." She shifted her eyes to my chest and took in a deep breath then let it out. "Growing up watching this show, I looked at Luke as the ideal man. He was always there for Lorelai, even when they were just friends. Even when he was angry with her. He's truly perfect. I always wanted someone like him." Her mouth curled up into a shy smile as she met my gaze again. "And now I've found someone like him."

Her eyes widened when I laughed out loud and she started to pull back. I wrapped my hand around her shoulder and held her in place.

"No, I'm not laughing at what you said. I mean, I am, but not for the reason you think." I kissed her forehead. "During the whole show, I kept thinking about how our relationship is so similar to Luke and Lorelai's."

"Really?"

I nodded.

"The only thing Luke did wrong was lose the woman he loved because of misunderstandings and miscommunications. I'm not gonna let that happen."

She blinked. Then blinked again.

Since I opened that door, I should walk through.

I slid my hand over to stroke her cheek.

"I love you, Keera."

A tear slowly slid down her cheek and she sucked in a sharp breath.

"Oh Simon, I love you, too."

She lunged forward and wrapped her arms around my neck then pressed her mouth against mine.

This isn't what I expected to happen tonight, but I have to say, I'm pretty happy it did.

CHAPTER 23

Keera

"You have a little bounce to your step," Anjannette said when I walked into the studio.

"I feel *so* much better. Thank you for insisting I take a second night off."

"You deserve it."

"How'd everything go?"

"Classes went well and the routines are all coming along."

"I'm just glad my uterus decided to wage a war on me during the week so I didn't miss today's beginners' class."

She didn't say anything to that, but just narrowed her eyes.

"Something happened," she said. "You look different."

I nibbled at my bottom lip, trying to control the smile that was fighting to take over my face.

"Simon told me he loves me."

She screeched.

"Oh honey, that's so awesome." She moved to hug me then froze. "You said it back, right?"

I rolled my eyes.

"Yes, I said it back."

"Just checking." She pulled me into her arms. "I'm happy for you."

"I'm happy too." Anjannette released me and stepped back. "I honestly never thought I could be this happy."

"I understand that, but trust me, you'll get used to it," she said with a smile.

Students started to arrive and I sat at the desk to check them in.

Zoe and Sacha walked in and approached me.

"You're all checked in," I said.

"I thought I was in pretty good shape, but I was so sore last week," Zoe said.

"You are in great shape, you just used different muscles."

"Hopefully tonight will be easier."

I scrunched my nose and they both groaned.

"Go stretch. That will help."

They went and joined the rest of the ladies as they stretched on the floor. The last few

students arrived and I closed the laptop and stood. Anjannette looked over the room then walked over to me.

"That's everyone, right?"

"Yep, the gang's all here."

"Let's get started then."

Last week we practiced climbing, had them get comfortable walking around the pole, and taught them how to do different versions of the step-around spin. Today, we're adding a back bend at the end of the step-around then we'll show them the fireman spin. If there's time, we'll introduce a fan kick.

We started off with some warm-up exercises, then got to it. Using the instructor's pole, I demonstrated the basics of climbing again.

"Okay, group one started last week, so group two, grab a pole and give it a try," I said.

Starting at opposite ends of the room, Anjannette and I gave tips as the ladies tried to climb the pole with different levels of success.

"Group one, you're up," Anjannette said after a few minutes.

After the poles were wiped down, the groups switched.

"Remember, squeeze the pole between your knees and push up," I said.

Again, they all gave it their best shot, but in the end, no one made it to the top. None of them gave up though, which is a good sign for future tricks. It's only going to get more difficult as we go on. But this seems like a great group of ladies. They've been cheering each other on and really seem to be enjoying themselves.

By the end of class, they'd all pretty much perfected the fireman spin and at least got to try the fan kick. Since this is the last class of the day, we told them they could stay and practice for a little while. Sophie and Eve are coming in to work on their routine, but that's not for another hour.

About half stayed. Most were interested in climbing. Which I get. I was obsessed with it when I started too.

"Keera, could you watch and make sure I'm doing this right?" Sacha asked.

I watched her mount, then try to climb. *Try* being the operative word. Using the pole next to her, I showed her what to do again.

"You want to put your grip higher and keep the pole between your knees and squeeze as you push up." I demonstrated what I just said, then did it again, moving up some more before sliding back down. "Now you try."

She was able to move up a little but just couldn't hold on.

"Shit, that hurts."

"Your skin will get used to it," I said.

She looked down at the *pole kisses* dotting her shins and the inside of her knees. I rarely get the bruises anymore, but my body was covered with them when I first started.

"I hope so," she said with a chuckle.

"Get some arnica cream. It really does help."

"I'm gonna give it another try," Zoe said.

Sacha and I stepped back to give her space.

She placed her shin against the pole and pushed up, squeezed her knees together, and pushed up a tiny bit more.

"Keep going," I said.

Inch by inch, she moved up to the middle of the pole. She wrapped her arms around it and hung there, laughing.

"At this rate, it'll take me a week to get to the top."

"You're doing great."

She let out a groan and slid down to the floor.

"You and Anjannette make it look so easy," she said, shaking out her legs and massaging her palms.

"Remember, we've been doing this a *long* time," I said. "It took me weeks to do what you just did, and almost two months to climb to the top of the pole. So trust me when I say, you're doing great."

"My hands are killing me. I'm done," she said to Sacha. "I'm going to go get dressed."

"I want to do a couple more spins," Sacha said.

Zoe said her goodbyes then walked out of the studio. I followed, hoping to get her alone. Before she entered the dressing room, I called her name.

"Can I talk to you for a second?"

"Sure. What's up?"

I've thought about how to bring this up, but decided the best thing to do is just say it.

"This is kind of a random thing to mention, but I wanted to let you know that Simon and I are dating."

"Oh wow." Her eyes widened. "That's great. How long have you guys been together?"

"About a month. It's pretty new, but I really like him."

It's strange to think it's been such a short time because I feel like we've been together forever.

"Understandable," she said. "He's an amazing guy."

"Yeah, he is."

"That's really awesome. I wish you two the best."

"Thank you. I appreciate that."

She seemed sincere. I thought this whole exchange was going to be awkward, but it really hasn't been. Of course, now I have no idea of what else to say. Thankfully Sacha approached so I didn't have to come up with anything.

SIMON

"So you're telling me that Shannon is moving home," Andrew said.

"Apparently."

"Holy shit."

He popped a piece of sushi into his mouth and chewed thoughtfully. I don't have to wonder what he's thinking. With Shannon living in the same ZIP code as him, he's wondering if he might have a chance with her.

"Are your parents happy?" Archer asked.

I'm not surprised he asked that. He's pretty close with his mom and I don't know what she'd do if he moved away. He didn't even go away to college.

"Yeah, I guess."

"Are you both going to be living here?" Andrew asked.

"For a little while. I'm going to start looking for an apartment, or maybe a house, after the holidays and I doubt Shannon will live here long." I shook my head. "I still can't believe she's moving back. So who knows what she'll do?"

"With the housing market so high, you're going to want to take your time if you're looking to buy a house," Archer said.

Then he went on to recite housing market statistics for the past six months and predictions for the next six.

"He's right," Andrew said. "There's really no reason to rush. Your parents will be gone again after the holidays. And even if they were going to be here, they're so cool, it's not a big deal."

"Plus, you'll be able to come over and gawk at Shannon while she's living here," I said.

Andrew opened his mouth, but the doorbell rang before any words came out.

"Who could that be?" Archer asked.

"No idea." I stood and walked over to open the door. "Keera, hi. This is a nice surprise."

"Sorry to just pop in."

"No, don't be." I gestured toward the boxes she was holding. "Do you need help with those?"

She handed them to me and I stepped aside to let her come inside.

"I know it's your game night, but today's Rosa's birthday

and her husband dropped off a ton of cupcakes and cookies, so I figured I'd bring some over for you and the guys."

"Wow, thanks."

We walked into the kitchen. Keera's already met my friends, so no introductions were needed. They said hello as I set the boxes on the table.

"Keera brought dessert," I said then turned my attention back to Keera. "Have a seat. There's plenty of sushi."

"Oh no, I just wanted to drop off the dessert. I don't want to break up your night."

"Stay and help us finish the sushi. We ordered way too much."

Surprisingly that came from Archer. He and Keera hit it off when they met at Poor Richards a couple weeks ago. Apparently he likes her enough to interrupt game night, and that's saying a lot with him.

I got Keera a plate and set it down in front of her. She grabbed a pair of chopsticks from the stack in the middle of the table.

"It should have told us something when the restaurant gave us eight pairs of chopsticks with our order," I said with a chuckle.

"That happens to my friends and me all the time. Apparently they think a serving of sushi is on par with a serving of potato chips," Keera said, as she used her chopsticks to transfer rolls to her plate.

"Weren't you supposed to have a private lesson after class?" I asked.

"Phoebe's sick so she cancelled." She popped a piece of sushi into her mouth and chewed. "I'm sorry she's not feeling well, but it's kind of nice to have the time off."

"I can imagine. You've been putting in a lot of hours lately," I said.

"That's because of the recital, right?" Andrew asked.

"Yeah, I have at least one private lesson every night after class."

"Did you get tickets yet?" he asked me.

"They're not on sale yet," I said, then looked at Keera. "Right?"

She finished chewing then swallowed and took a drink.

"Right. Next week. I'd grab some for you early, but since they're sold electronically, I can't." She smiled at me. "You know all about those pesky computer systems."

"That I do."

Keera shifted her eyes between Andrew and Archer.

"Are you guys coming to the recital?"

"I am," Andrew said.

"I don't think so."

She picked up a piece of spicy tuna roll with her chopsticks.

"You're gonna miss out on the best show of the year," she said to Archer, then popped it into her mouth.

"I'm not sure I'd be comfortable."

"It's just dancing."

"As time goes on, you'll realize there's a lot Archer isn't comfortable with, but we love him anyway."

"Well, I hope you decide to come," Keera said to him. "But if you don't, at least come out to the after party."

"Where's that going to be?" I asked.

"I'm not sure. Last year we went to Poor Richards."

That led to a discussion of potential places to go. While we listed the pluses and minuses of each spot, we managed to finish the sushi and started to dig into dessert.

"I've already had way too many sweets, so I'm going to take off. Thank you for sharing your sushi and allowing me to butt in on your game night."

Keera stood and started to collect the empty plates.

"Don't worry about it," I said. "We'll clean up."

"Are you sure?"

"Positive."

"All right then." She picked up her purse. "I'll see you guys later. Thanks again. It was fun."

The guys said goodbye and I walked Keera to the door.

"I'm so glad you came over. It was a nice surprise."

I wrapped my arms around her and she draped hers over my shoulders.

"It was fun."

Leaning down, I pressed my mouth against hers but since we have an audience, I kept it short.

"Text me when you get home."

"Will do."

She gave me another quick kiss, then stepped back. I opened the door and watched as she walked to the driveway, got into her car, and drove away.

I went back into the kitchen and joined Andrew and Archer at the table.

"These cupcakes are amazing," Andrew said.

I reached for a Linzer cookie and took a big bite.

Archer pulled the box closer and perused its contents for longer than I thought was necessary before picking up a chocolate chip cookie.

"Let me know when you're ordering the tickets for the recital. I might want to go," he said before taking a bite.

Andrew and I looked at each other, eyes wide. Keera must have really worked her magic on Archer for him to even think about changing his mind. It's not something that usually happens.

"Will do."

CHAPTER 24

Keera

Anjannette and I sat on the floor watching Sophie and Eve go through their routine. We're two weeks away from the recital and have both been staying for all the lessons and practices. Two sets of eyes are always better than one at catching any outstanding issues or potential tweaks.

We both clapped as the song came to an end and the ladies finished their final spins.

"Yaaassss!" Anjannette said.

"You guys look awesome!" I said.

They grabbed drinks and joined us on the floor.

"I'm still not spinning as fast as Sophie, but I'm trying," Eve said.

"And I keep messing up that one spot," Sophie added.

"Some of your spins are a little out of sync and a couple transitions need to be smoother, but other than that you look great," I said.

"Don't forget that we're sitting here watching, specifically looking for issues, and you know what you're supposed to be doing. So if you mess up, it seems like a glaring error. But people just watching the show won't pick up on any small imperfections in your routine. It really looks great. You did an amazing job putting it together."

"Thanks to Keera," Sophie said.

"I just made some suggestions. You guys ran with it."

We chatted for a few more minutes, then Eve stood.

"Well ladies, as fun as this is, I'm going to head out. It's been a long week and I'm exhausted."

"I need to go too," Sophie said, then bobbed her eyebrows. "I have a hot date."

We said our goodbyes and Anjannette and I coordinated schedules for the upcoming week.

"I'm so glad we decided to take Sundays off," I said.

"Me too. I'm looking forward to just chilling with Leo tomorrow," she said. "You're meeting Simon's parents, right?"

"Yeah, they got home last night and his mom invited me over for dinner tomorrow." I glanced at the clock. "That reminds me. I have to stop at the store on the way home. I'm making cinnamon apple cupcakes with salted caramel icing and I need a few things."

"Hopefully you're going to save a couple for your bestie."

I laughed at the pathetic look she gave me.

"Of course. I'll bring some in for you on Monday." I checked myself out in the mirror. "I look like crap. I'm sure I'll run into everyone I know at the store."

"You look fine." She grabbed her bags and swung them over her shoulder.

I know that's not true but I thanked her anyway.

We locked up and headed out to the parking lot.

"Good luck tomorrow. Let me know how it goes."

"Will do. See you Monday."

Stopping at the store is the last thing I feel like doing, but if I don't, I'll have to go early tomorrow. And I know I'll want to do it even less then. Thankfully it's on the way home.

There aren't many cars in the parking lot, so hopefully I can get in and out in the blink of an eye. I mentally went over my list as I walked into the store and grabbed a basket. After picking up apples, brown sugar, and flour, I stopped at the dairy section for heavy cream. I'm not sure of our egg situation so I added a dozen to the basket before making my way to the front of the store.

I was a few steps from the checkout line when I heard Brian's voice. My stomach twisted and a feeling of panic washed over me before I reminded myself that he's not part of my life any longer and can't affect me. I enjoyed the sense of relief for a second before mentally beating myself up for having such a shitty reaction in the first place. Then I gave myself a pass since this is the first time I'm seeing him in person since we broke up.

All that happened in the short time between hearing his voice and turning to see him walking toward me. By the time he was next to me, I had my emotions under control. Mostly.

"Keera," he said. "It's been a while."

"Brian."

He followed me to the check-out and I felt his eyes on me as I placed my items on the conveyor belt. Of course I'd run into *him* when I look like crap. I fought the urge to fidget with my hair or suck in my stomach. Old habits die hard, unfortunately. It just sucks that I ever formed those habits in the first place.

Supposedly the opposite of love isn't hate, it's indifference, but I'm not sure I'll ever get to the point where the thought of the five years I wasted with him won't make my blood boil.

"I heard you got laid off from Wilder." I nodded. "What are you doing now?"

The cashier finished checking out the person in front of me, giving me a reason to ignore Brian's question. I hyper-focused on the woman as she scanned and bagged my items. After paying, I grabbed the bag then half turned and nodded at Brian before heading toward the door.

As I walked to my car, I mentally patted myself on the back for handling the situation so well. Yes, I had some thoughts and reactions I wish I didn't, but at least I kept it cool on the outside.

I just placed my hand on my door handle when I heard him call my name again.

"Hey, wait up."

Taking in a calming breath, I let it out slowly as he approached and raised my right brow.

"You're not going to even say anything?" he asked.

"What do you want me to say?"

"I asked you a question. An answer would be nice."

"I'm working at the pole studio."

"What are you doing for a full-time job?"

"That *is* my full-time job."

He shook his head and let out a chuckle. That's my cue to leave. I don't want to get into this with him and don't have any reason to. I opened my door and tossed the bag into the passenger seat.

"That's it? You're just leaving?"

"I need to get home. I have things to do."

"You don't want to get a drink? Get caught up?"

In the past, the smile he flashed would have had me halfway to orgasm, but now it just looks smarmy. I'll consider that progress.

"No, I'm beat."

"Maybe some other time?"

"I don't think that's a good idea."

I thought about adding "thanks" or "see you" but I wouldn't mean either.

"*I* think we should get together and discuss *getting together*."

I looked at him and blinked. Multiple times. I'm not even sure what to say to that. There's a lot I *can* say, but I decided to leave him with two things.

"I'm seeing someone," I said. "And I said everything I needed to when we broke up."

Wanting to get out of here before things get nasty...and history has taught me they will...I settled behind the steering wheel. Brian stepped forward, so I couldn't close the door. Resting his elbow against the roof of the car, he bent down invading my space. His eyes took another tour of my body.

"Remember, nice tits and great blowjobs only keep a guy happy for so long. You need to get in better shape or he'll lose interest eventually. No man wants to date a girl who weighs more than him."

I reached out, grabbed the handle, and pulled, banging the door against his hip. He jumped back and I slammed it shut. With shaking hands, I pressed the ignition button, shifted the car into reverse, and pulled out of my spot.

I've come a long way since we broke up, but his words

still sting. Blinking back tears as I drove the short distance home, I fought to keep them from sinking into my head.

SIMON

"NEED HELP WITH ANYTHING?"

My mom finished rolling a slice of prosciutto and added it to the stack sitting on the board in front of her.

"The potatoes are next on my list if you want to start on them."

I grabbed a knife from the block and a spoon from the drawer and walked over to the other side of the island. After cutting one of the enormous potatoes in half, I scooped out its contents and put them into a bowl, then did the same with the other three.

"I'm making asparagus. Should I make a salad, too?"

"I don't think we need a salad."

"Are you sure?"

"I'm sure."

My mom had fried and chopped bacon earlier and I picked it up and tossed it in the bowl with the potatoes. After grabbing cheddar cheese and sour cream from the refrigerator, I added some of each to the mixture and stirred. These stuffed, twice-baked potatoes are my favorite. My mouth is watering just thinking about digging into one.

"You look happy," she said

I added some more cheese before looking over at her.

"I am."

"Do you think she's the one?" she asked. "I know the

relationship is relatively new, but let's face it, when you know, you know."

After all the ingredients were combined, I started spooning the mixture back into the empty potato skins.

"I always thought she was the one. We just needed to get our timing right."

Before she could react to that, the doorbell rang. I wiped my hands and went to answer.

"Hi."

I gave Keera a quick kiss as she entered then closed the door behind her. She held up the box in her hands.

"I brought cupcakes."

"That's the second time you've shown up here with dessert. You know you're setting a precedent, right?"

She smiled at my words as I took the box, but it didn't quite reach her eyes.

"It smells really good in here."

"My mom is making her famous cheddar and chive popovers."

"Sounds yummy."

"They are. You're gonna love them."

As we approached the kitchen, the smell got even stronger and as we entered, I realized

it's because my mom just removed the items in question out of the oven. She looked over at us and smiled as she set the pan on the counter.

"Mom, this is Keera. Keera, this is my mom, Lily."

"It's so nice to meet you," my mom said as she removed her oven mitt.

"Nice to meet you, Mrs. Parker. I've heard so much about you through the years."

"I've heard a lot about you too, and please call me Lily."

"Keera brought cupcakes," I said as I set the box on the island.

My mom opened the lid and peeked into the box.

"They look amazing and smell even better," she said. "What kind are they?"

"Apple cinnamon with salted caramel icing."

"Maybe we should eat dessert first." Keera and I looked at each other and laughed. "What's so funny?" Mom asked.

"I had dinner with Keera's family a few weeks ago and brought Smidgens and caramel apples, and her mom said the same thing."

"Great minds think alike," she said, adding the popovers to the charcuterie board. "It's such a beautiful day, especially for this time of year, so I thought we'd eat out on the patio. If it gets cold, we can fire up the heaters."

"Sounds perfect," Keera said. "Do you need help with anything?"

"No, I think I'm good. Simon's dad is outside fussing with the grill. Let's head out there." She picked up the charcuterie board and looked at me. "Grab the potatoes."

Keera followed my mom out the door and I walked over and picked up the platter, then joined them.

"Your house is so beautiful," Keera said to my parents as I stepped outside.

"Thank you," Mom said. "After living in the RV for so long, it feels like a mansion."

"Which is a good thing, because after next week both kids will be living here with us," Dad added.

"That's right," Keera said. "Are you happy Shannon is moving back?"

"I'm happy if she's happy," Mom said.

"You'll only be here a couple months with us anyway," I said. "Then you're hitting the road again."

My parents shared a look and dad shrugged.

"We'll see," he said.

I opened my mouth to question that, but my mom interrupted.

"Why don't you start on the charcuterie," she said. "Keera, what would you like to drink? I have an amazing Syrah from Napa. There's also beer. Or if you want something nonalcoholic, I have iced tea or lemonade."

"I'll have a glass of wine with dinner, but for now, water is fine."

My mom disappeared into the house and Keera and I settled at the table.

"Everything okay?" I asked.

She looked at me out of the corner of her eye and nodded.

"Yeah, I'm just tired. It's been a long week."

With the schedule she's been working, I've no doubt she's tired, but beyond that, something just seems...off. She seems flat, like she's just going through the motions. But I'm not going to badger her about it right now.

I placed my hand over hers and squeezed.

"In a few weeks, things will be back to normal."

She took in a deep breath and pasted on a smile as my mom returned with the drinks. Both she and my dad joined us at the table.

We talked about plans for Thanksgiving and picked at the charcuterie board. Her family has an early dinner and mine eats later, so we planned on spending the day together.

"Unless you just want to hang out with your family and we'll see each other Saturday for the concert."

What is that about? We've already discussed this. And if we didn't spend Thanksgiving together, why wouldn't we do something on Friday? We've already planned on spending the whole holiday weekend with each other.

"No, we can keep our original plan. It'll be nice to see your whole family again."

She nodded, but didn't say anything.

"Simon mentioned your father plays in Afternoon Delight," Dad said. "Lily and I used to follow them years ago."

"Oh wow." She looked at me. "You didn't mention that."

"I only recently found out myself."

"We're definitely going to the anniversary show," he said.

"That's great. It should be a fun night."

My parents discussed how long it's been since they saw the band. After much

debate, they decided on twenty years.

"I'm really looking forward to it," Dad said.

"I hate their name, but they do put on an awesome show," Keera said.

"Their name is why we went to see them in the first place," Mom added.

Keera groaned.

"When I was a teenager, I was mortified when my friends found out my dad played in the band. Of course he knew that and made it a point to mention it whenever they were around."

My parents laughed at that.

"Shannon used to get embarrassed because her friends all thought John was cute."

"Hey, I'm still cute," he said.

"Of course you are." She patted his back and stood. "Why don't you take your cute self over and throw the steaks on the grill? I'm going to fetch more drinks."

"Your parents are amazing," she said, once they were both out of earshot.

"Yeah they are." I kissed her forehead. "So are you."

She sniffed and I pulled back and looked into her glistening eyes.

"And you are very sweet."

Her words are right and her smile is more genuine, but something still seems off. But I'm sure she'll share what's going on eventually.

CHAPTER 25

Keera

"Okay spill. What's going on with you?" Anjannette asked as we left the studio.

"Why?"

"You haven't been yourself all week."

I thought about giving her the "I'm tired" line Simon has been hearing, but I don't think she'll buy it any more than he seems to be.

"When I stopped at the store last week, I ran into Brian."

"*Fuck.*"

We got into my car and I got my thoughts together as I pulled out of the parking lot. We're heading to Joyce's Café to meet Simon and Leo, who've been there for the past couple hours watching the Notre Dame game. We planned ahead to be their designated drivers. I drove Anjannette to the studio earlier so she'll take Leo home in their car. Archer doesn't drink so he brought Andrew and Simon.

It's only a fifteen-minute drive, so if I'm going to discuss this with Anjannette, I better start talking.

"He wanted to go for a drink and discuss 'getting together.' When I told him I was seeing someone and that I'd said all I needed to when we broke up, he got nasty." I stopped at a red light and turned to face her. "He said, and I quote, 'Remember, nice tits and great blowjobs only keep a guy happy for so long. You need to get in better shape or he'll lose interest eventually. No man wants to date a girl who weighs more than him.'"

"What a fucking piece of shit." She grabbed my forearm and squeezed. "You know that's not true, right?"

My answer pisses me off and I know she'll feel the same way. The light turned green and I drove a couple blocks without answering.

"*Keera*. Please tell me you're not letting that douchebag into your head."

I shook my head.

"I know how Brian works."

"That didn't answer my question."

I took in a deep breath and let it out.

"I'd be lying if I said his words didn't affect me at all. And besides making me angry, that makes me wonder if it's really behind me. If I'm ready to be in a relationship."

"You *are* in a relationship, and it's a *great* one," she said. "Simon is really wonderful and you two are perfect together."

"I know he is."

I just can't help but wonder if he should be with someone better than me. But I didn't say that because I really don't want to discuss it. Plus Anjannette would probably freak out.

We didn't say anything else the rest of the way to Joyce's. I lucked out and found a parking spot right in front and backed in.

"Please don't give what Brian said another thought," Anjannette said as we walked through the front door.

I tell myself that every time his words creep into my mind. Hopefully at some point I'll listen.

We found Simon, Andrew, Archer, and Leo sitting at a table in the corner in the back room. None of them seemed to be paying attention to the football game that had the rest of the crowd entranced. Simon spotted us as we approached them.

He looked at Leo and stood.

"Our ladies have arrived."

Simon kissed me then pulled out the chair next to him.

"Thanks," I said as I sat. "How's it going?"

Before he could answer, the crowd cheered and a few seconds later a song started playing in the background. The guys picked up their glasses and toasted, then chugged their beer. Well, Simon, Andrew, and Leo chugged beer. Archer drank what looked like Sprite.

"They play the Notre Dame fight song whenever the team scores a touchdown," Leo said.

Anjannette and I looked at each other and shrugged.

"Are you hungry?" Simon asked.

"Starving."

Even though he directed the question to me, Anjannette answered too.

"Do you want me to grab some menus?"

"Nope. I have it memorized," I said.

"So do I," Anjannette said.

When the waitress dropped off a pitcher of beer at the

table next to us, Simon waved her over. Anjannette and I rattled off our orders.

"Another round?" she asked and reached for the empty glasses.

"You're swamped," Simon said. "I'll take these to the bar and get more drinks."

"Thanks. I'll get this out to you as soon as I can," she said to Anjannette and me. "It's pretty crazy in the kitchen so it might take a little extra time."

"No worries," I said.

"What would you like to drink?" Simon asked.

"I just want water," I said.

"Water is good for me," Anjannette added.

"Another round?" he asked the guys.

"Why not?" Leo said, then put his arm around Anjannette's shoulders and squeezed. "I have my designated driver to bring me home."

"I'll have another one. My designated driver is here, too," Andrew said, making a kiss-y face toward Archer.

"Would you behave?" Archer said as he shook his head.

"Let's go grab more beer and a pitcher of water," Simon said to Leo.

They stood and walked toward the bar, looking a little off balance, but not totally stumbling. When Anjannette and Leo got together, I decided I wanted a relationship like theirs. And now I have one. I just have to make sure I don't let past insecurities screw it up.

Simon

. . .

"This gameday special is the most awesome thing," Leo said. "Thanks for inviting me to come along."

"Anytime," I said.

"I celebrated my twenty-first birthday here during a Notre Dame game," Andrew said.

"And he got really, really drunk." I said.

When Notre Dame plays, Joyce's has a special that includes all-you-can-eat burgers and all-you-can-drink beer for just $15. It's definitely a bargain.

Keera and Anjannette's food arrived and they dug right in.

"So what's everyone doing for Thanksgiving?" Leo asked.

Archer was the first to answer.

"I'm going to my aunt's house."

"I go to my grandparents'," Andrew said. "But I'm on call, so we'll see if I make it through dinner."

"We'll be at my grandmother's in the early afternoon and Simon's parents later in the day," Keera said before taking a bite of a mozzarella stick.

She seems more like herself today and her matter-of-fact answer about what we're doing for the holiday is reassuring. Maybe she *was* just tired this past week.

"What about you two?" I asked.

"We're spending it with my family in New Jersey."

"I'm bummed you guys won't be at the concert Saturday night," Keera said.

"Me too," Anjannette said. "I love going to see your dad's band play."

"We can always sneak out early," Leo said.

"I don't want to ruin your Thanksgiving," she said.

He smiled at her and said, "As long as I'm with you, it'll be perfect."

The crowd let out a collective groan and we turned our attention to the TV. Archer explained the missed pass that had everyone so upset, then proceeded to explain the physics behind its lack of completion. I'm sure if a sports team ever heard some of his breakdowns, they'd hire him on the spot.

We hung out for a little while longer, before deciding to head out. Anjannette gave Keera a hug and we all said goodbye and I watched them walk down the block toward their cars before turning back to Keera.

"Nice spot," I said as we stood next to Keera's car right in front of us.

"Nothing but the best."

She opened the door and gestured for me to get in.

"Thank you, ma'am."

I flopped into the passenger seat and chuckled.

"You good?" Keera asked.

"Never better."

She smiled then closed the door and I watched her walk around the front of the car before getting in and settling behind the wheel.

With my head against the seat, I looked over at her.

"What?" Keera asked when she noticed me staring at her.

"You're beautiful."

She rested her hand on my cheek and leaned forward to give me a kiss. After pulling back just enough to look me in the eye, she asked, "How drunk are you?"

"Mmm, I just have a buzz. Why?"

"Well, Granny Vi is at her Friendsgiving tonight and won't be home until later."

"So what are you saying?"

"I thought we could go back to my house where we'll be

alone. But I don't want to take advantage of you if you're drunk." she said with a smirk.

"Can you take advantage of the willing?"

That smirk turned into a full-blown laugh as she started the car and pulled onto the street.

CHAPTER 26

Keera

WE RAN UP THE DRIVEWAY AND I FUMBLED WITH THE KEYS IN my rush to get into the house. When I finally got the door open, we dashed inside and Simon slammed it closed behind us, then backed me up, pinning me against it with his body.

"I feel like I haven't touched you in forever."

He slid his hands down to cup my ass and squeezed, tilting my hips against his erection. I let out a low groan when he pressed his lips against mine then wrapped my arms around his neck, melting into his hard body as our tongues met. I matched his tongue stroke for stroke and he tightened his hold, pulling me onto my tiptoes as he opened his mouth wider, deepening the kiss.

It went on and on, our mouths feasting, tongues tangling in perfect rhythm. All my senses focused on Simon. His taste, smell, and feel consumed me and I wanted more.

But not here.

Simon's gaze met mine as I ended the kiss.

"Let's head upstairs," I said.

Taking his hand, I led him up to my room.

"What time will Granny Vi be home?" Simon asked as we walked toward the bed, shedding clothes along the way.

"She'll be out until at least eleven. So that gives us three hours. Think that's enough time?" I asked as I removed my bra and tossed it to the floor.

His eyes focused on what I'd just exposed and he slowly shook his head.

"I'm not sure, but I'll give it my best shot."

After removing his jeans and boxer briefs, he walked toward me. I straightened and sucked in my stomach as he placed his hands on either side of my waist.

"I've never had a guy in here before, so this is extra exciting."

His hands slowly stroked up to cup my breasts. Sensation zinged down to my clit when he brushed his thumbs across my nipples.

"No?"

I shook my head.

"Granted, my official childhood room is at my parents' house, but I spent enough time here that I think it kind of counts." I shrugged. "Regardless, we're christening the room."

He shifted his hands to my ass and stepped forward, pulling me against his erection.

"If we only have a few hours, we better move this along." Leaning down, he nibbled at my earlobe then his warm breath caressed my ear. "And you're not nearly naked enough."

"I'm standing here in nothing but underwear."

"That's way too much."

Looping his fingers into the waistband of the item in question, he pushed them down my thighs until gravity took hold and they fell to the floor. I stepped out of the scrap of lace as he took my hands and led me to the bed.

He followed me onto the mattress and we met in the middle. I reached down to wrap my hand around his cock, but he intertwined his fingers with mine and pulled me forward. My aching nipples dragged across his chest as he shifted on top of me and pressed my arms above my head. Lowering his head, he took my mouth in a kiss that was hot, desperate, and all-consuming. I wrapped my leg around his hips and swallowed Simon's groan as his dick pressed against my slick folds.

His hands shifted to my waist and he released my mouth then rolled us until I was on top, straddling his waist. Before I got settled, he wrapped his hands around my elbows and pulled me forward until my thighs rested against his chest.

I started to shift back to press against his cock, but he grabbed my ass to hold me in place.

"Not that way. Come here," he said, nudging me forward.

My eyes widened when I realized his intent.

"Simon, I can't do *that*."

Somehow my words came out as both a whisper and a shriek.

"Why not?"

"I'll suffocate you."

The corner of his mouth kicked up in a sexy smirk.

"What a way to go."

He shifted down until his shoulders rested flat against the mattress, but his head remained slightly propped up on the pillow. Still holding my ass, he pulled me forward until my knees tipped over his shoulders and my calves straddled his biceps.

My thigh muscles strained as I held myself back, just inches above his face.

"Relax."

I met his lust-filled gaze and realized that he really wants this. I nodded and took in a deep breath then let it out slowly, trying my best to do what he's asking. Finally some of the tension left my thighs and I dropped closer. Simon lifted his head and licked me from back to front, lingering on my clit at every pass.

"Oh God."

Simon

Keera slammed her hand against the headboard and all the tension left her thighs as she tilted forward. Bending my elbows, I rested my hands on her hips and pulled her even closer to give her a good tongue fucking.

Her moans echoed through the room, urging me to keep going. Not that I want to stop. I've dreamed about being with her like this for years, and it's even more amazing than I imagined.

My whispered name sounded like a desperate plea, and I looked up and met her gaze. Eating her sweet pussy with her watching takes things to a whole other level.

I licked and sucked, feasting on her until one orgasm crashed through her, which as far as I'm concerned is just a good start.

"Simon!"

She leaned back and rested her hands on my waist, thrusting herself into my face, opening her fully to me.

Perfect. I tickled her clit with the tip of my tongue then nibbled before fully drawing it into my mouth and sucking.

Keera's legs trembled as another orgasm crashed through her and more of her weight settled against me. I wanted to go for a third, but her hands twisted into my hair.

"No more," she panted. "I can't–"

She shook her head and sucked in a breath.

Shifting up onto the pillow, I pulled her down until her head rested against my chest. Her breathing slowed and I thought maybe she'd fallen asleep so it surprised me when she wiggled then pressed against my throbbing erection.

"We should do something about this."

Before I could process her words, she moved down until her face was even with my cock. She tucked her hair behind her ear then leaned forward and dragged her tongue from base to tip before swirling it around and sucking at the tip, slamming me right against the edge.

"Keera."

My voice came out as a strangled croak. She looked up at me through her lashes then slowly slid down, taking me all the way to the back of her throat. The look of pure bliss on her face was more than I could handle so I closed my eyes and focused on breathing in an attempt to get myself under control.

If Keera stopped what she was doing, that might have worked, but she didn't. She kept moving up and down, settling into a slow rhythm, designed to drive me insane. I groaned as she increased the pace, taking me deeper and deeper with each pass.

"You're killing me, you know that?"

I was surprised to string that sentence together with so much blood rushing from my brain to my dick. She didn't miss a beat at my words, and her sly smile didn't look the least bit apologetic.

Curling my fingers into her hair, I gave her a warning.

"Keera, you need to stop."

She released me with an audible pop and smiled.

"Just relax and enjoy."

How could I argue with that?

Taking my cock into her mouth again, she licked and sucked, her tongue twirling at each pass. I did everything I could to stop my release, but when she wrapped her hand around the base and pumped in perfect rhythm with her mouth, I couldn't hold it back any longer.

"*Keera.*"

I barely recognized my own voice as my orgasm crashed through me.

She stayed with me until I was totally spent then slowly pushed back. Shifting to the side, she rested her head against my chest as my heartbeat returned to normal. Once it did, she propped up on her elbow and looked down at me.

"I have to say, as far as a christening goes, that was pretty spectacular."

"Can't argue with that."

I shifted my gaze down and took a lazy tour of her curves, wondering if I could recover quickly enough to do it again before Granny Vi gets home. With my parents at home, planning alone time is much more complicated. And it's only going to get worse when Shannon moves back. I've already approached a realtor to speed up my house search. Hopefully when I find one, I'll be able to convince Keera to move in with me.

"What?" she asked when our eyes met again.

That last thought isn't something I want to discuss just yet, so I shared just part of what I'm thinking.

"I have two thoughts. One, I need to find a house sooner rather than later so we can have some privacy without working around other people's schedules. And two, I'm hoping the little guy has enough stamina to do this one more time before your grandmother gets home."

Her eyes shifted down to the body part in question then she met my gaze again, her brow raised.

"There's nothing *little* about him," she said, tracing her finger from base to tip, causing him to twitch. "And I have complete faith that you can do it one more time."

CHAPTER 27

Keera

I FINISHED LOADING THE DISHWASHER, ADDED A POD, CLOSED the door, and turned it on. After wiping down the counter, I dried my hands and looked around the kitchen.

"We did a good job, ladies," I said.

"For just seven people, we had a *lot* of food," my sister-in-law Anna said.

"It seems like there's more every year," Mom added.

"And then we get to enjoy the leftovers all weekend. Which is kind of the best part."

I looked over at the leftover containers lined up on the counter. Some are for Kevin and Anna and others will go home with Mom and Dad. The rest will stay here with Granny Vi and me.

"What time are you and Simon leaving?" Mom asked.

"I think dinner is at five, so we still have some time."

Mom directed my attention to the dining room table where Granny Vi was showing Simon old photo albums.

"She must really like him if she's doing that," she said then looked at Anna. "The only girlfriend of Kevin's she showed them to is you."

"Kevin had other girlfriends?" Anna asked, looking shocked.

"None that mattered." Mom said, giving her a quick hug as she walked out of the kitchen.

Anna looked at me.

"Simon is really great."

I looked over at our topic of conversation as he looked at my mom, who sat down across from him at the dining room table.

"Yeah, he is."

Since that weird week after I saw Brian, things have been back to normal between us. And any issues we had were totally on me. Thankfully I was able to have a quick Zoom chat with Dr. Green. After I beat myself up for letting my ex get into my head, she reminded me that a lifetime of insecurities don't go away in a few months. She also urged me to discuss things with Simon, but I haven't done that and I'm not sure I will. As long as I can keep my shit together, there's no reason to.

Anna went to sit on the couch next to Kevin and I stayed in the kitchen a few minutes longer, watching Simon interact with my mom and grandmother.

Brian and I never spent holidays together. He'd do his thing and I'd do mine and sometimes we'd get together later. He never liked spending time with my family and anytime he did, he'd expect me to stick to his side. The only time I was next to Simon today was during dinner. Time to remedy that.

I walked into the dining room and sat next to him. Granny Vi was sitting on his other side showing him pictures from when I was in junior high, my peak Goth years. My mom chimed in as they judged my hair, clothes, and makeup choices.

If I'm being honest, my mom and Granny Vi made the comments. Simon just laughed.

"You know, payback is a bitch, and we're heading to your house shortly," I said to him.

He put his arm around my shoulder and pulled me closer to kiss the top of my head.

"I'm sure Shannon will enjoy showing you pictures of me in all my nerdy glory."

Pulling back, he smiled and if I wasn't already in love with him, I would have fallen at this very moment.

SIMON

"IF I EAT ONE MORE BITE, I'M GOING TO EXPLODE," KEERA said.

"You haven't even had dessert yet," Shannon said. "Mom makes the best pumpkin roll."

Keera groaned.

"I *love* pumpkin roll."

"You could always take some home if you don't make room for it now," Mom said.

"I appreciate that. Eating two Thanksgiving dinners isn't for the weak."

"We're glad you could join us." Dad returned from his office and she turned to him. "All done for the night?"

"Yep, that should be it."

When Shannon and I were younger, he was on the road a lot during football season, which included Thanksgiving and Christmas. Mom, Shannon, and I used to travel to wherever he was so we could spend the holidays together. His role has changed since then but, even though he's not reporting from games anymore, he still offers commentary and does interviews. Now his office is set up to do all that remotely.

"Is anyone else coming?" Shannon asked.

I've been so preoccupied with spending the day with Keera, I never even asked if any of my aunts, uncles, or cousins are joining us. Even if no one comes for dinner, often we have a houseful for dessert.

But that's different every year based on who's where. And as my generation starts their own families or moves away, the family gets more and more spread out.

"No, it's just us," Mom said. "Which is kind of nice, I think."

"With no one else here, I was wondering if you'd want to play some Madden," Dad said.

I looked at Keera.

"Don't worry about me. I'll be fine." She smiled. "I can pump your mom and Shannon for information about you. Maybe get them to show me some photo albums or home movies."

"Have at it." Leaning down, I gave her a quick kiss. "Or you can come downstairs and watch me kick my dad's ass."

"In your dreams," he said.

"Unless your mom needs help cleaning up, I'm gonna sit here and veg until I'm not so stuffed."

"Yes, let us sit here and digest so we can make room for dessert," Shannon said from the other end of the couch.

Now I get why Keera kept watching me earlier at her house. Her exes didn't do well when they were alone with her family so it was a novelty for her that I did. If I left Zoe for a second, there'd be some kind of issue I'd have to hear about later. This is much nicer.

I followed my dad down to the basement and fired up the ancient Playstation. We settled next to each other on the couch as the Madden graphics filled the screen. I felt my dad's eyes on me and I looked over at him before pressing start.

"I didn't say anything after we had dinner last week, but I really like Keera."

"Yeah, me too."

"So things are serious?" he asked as he started the game.

"Yeah, I'd say so."

This is how we had most of our heart-to-heart conversations through the years. Sitting next to each other playing Madden.

"In case you didn't remember, your grandmother left her engagement ring to you. It's in a safe deposit box at the bank."

He chuckled when I cursed under my breath as he blitzed my quarterback. I focused on the game as his words played through my mind.

Technically I knew about the ring, but haven't thought about it in a long time. And even though I dated Zoe for years, my dad never mentioned it. Which isn't surprising. After we broke up, my family told me they never thought we were right for each other. I'm guessing they would have spoken up sooner if I tried to take things to the next level.

I pictured my grandmother's ring in my mind and smiled. Even if I tried to give the ring to Zoe, she would have hated it. But the unique design is just Keera's style.

After I scored a touchdown, my dad looked over at me.

"So if you decide you want it, give me a little warning so I can go get it."

"Will do."

CHAPTER 28

Keera

"Your dad's band is amazing," Simon said against my ear.

I nodded and settled back against his chest.

Finnegan's has been crowded since Afternoon Delight started playing, but now, toward the end of their first set, it's totally packed. We got here super early to grab some tables close to the stage and have been here since. I don't plan on leaving this seat unless I have to go to the bathroom.

The final strains of "American Girl" finished and once the applause died down, Gus, the lead singer, announced they were taking a short break.

My dad joined us and I introduced him to Simon's parents.

"We used to follow you back in the day," John said. "I was so excited when Keera mentioned this."

"It's nice to meet you and I'm glad you could make it."

"I didn't realize you guys still play. Then again, I've traveled so much through the years, I lost touch."

"It's not a regular thing anymore, just a few times a year."

My phone buzzed.

This place is insane. Where are you?

"Anjannette is here," I said to Simon.

I looked around, but didn't see her.

We're all the way up front.

We found some pole people. I'll drag them along.

I saw Leo's head over the people standing near the bar and waved to catch his attention. He headed in our direction and soon I saw Anjannette behind him, followed by Sophie, Eve, Phoebe, Rosa, and Mason.

"I'm so happy you made it."

Anjannette gave me a quick hug.

"I really didn't want to miss this," she said, then looked over her shoulder at Leo. "Let's go say hi to Keera's dad. We'll be right back."

As they left, I looked at the rest of the gang.

"Thanks so much for coming."

I'd mentioned it at the studio, but honestly didn't think anyone would come.

We're not all going to fit at the table, but I think there's enough space around us for people to stand. We'll make it work somehow.

Some of the crowd had headed outside during the break, but had started slowly shuffling back in. I spotted Andrew and Archer walking in with them and waved.

"Sorry we're late," Archer said, then looked over at Andrew. "*He* was late."

"Excuse me if I had an emergency surgery."

"I know, you're saving lives." Archer rolled his eyes.

"You could have come without me."

Archer crossed his arms over his chest and shook his head.

"You're actually just in time for the second set," I said.

The band had taken the stage again and my dad started playing the *Jeopardy* theme as they waited for the house music to be turned off.

Anjannette and Leo joined us again.

"I'm gonna get a few pitchers of beer for the table," Leo said. "Does anyone want something different?"

"Grab some water too," I said. "I'm really thirsty and have been chugging too much beer."

All my pole peeps were okay with beer and Archer said he'd have water. Simon and Leo walked toward the bar just as the house music stopped. The crowd cheered as the band started to play the beginning strains of "Cover of the Rolling Stone" by Dr. Hook. The song is a fan favorite because every member of the band sings a part.

I was enjoying the music when I saw Archer do a double-take then frown.

He leaned down and said to Andrew, "What's *she* doing here?"

Following his gaze across the room, I spotted some of my beginner series ladies walking toward us, including Zoe. As she, Sacha, and Jill approached, I pasted a smile on my face and reminded myself that this is no big deal.

SIMON

I FOLLOWED LEO THROUGH THE CROWD, HOLDING TWO pitchers of beer in one hand and a stack of glasses in the other. As we approached the table and set everything down, I noticed Archer looking more aggravated than usual. Then I saw why. I glanced at Keera and cringed at her fake smile. I'm guessing she wasn't expecting Zoe to come tonight.

Either way, it's really not a big deal. They've been in each other's company for weeks now without an issue. Yes Zoe is an ex, but now she's just a friend. Sort of.

Leo filled a bunch of glasses with beer and Anjannette handed them out. When he was done, Leo grabbed one for himself and sat next to my dad. At the bar he told me he wanted to talk to him. How they're going to have a good conversation in here when it's so loud, I have no idea.

I filled a couple glasses with water then turned and handed one to Keera.

"Here you go," I said as I handed her the glass then gave the other one to Archer.

"Thank you." She took a sip, then gestured toward the women.

"Simon, this is Sacha and Jill. And you already know Zoe."

I barely heard her over the music and figured they wouldn't hear me either, but I nodded and said hello anyway.

The band played one awesome song after the other and the whole crowd was totally into the show, including our not-so-little group. Archer even seemed to be enjoying himself, which is surprising because loud music and crowds aren't his thing.

"We're gonna slow things down for a minute and I'll take a break while Marty takes the mic," Gus said.

Keera's dad stepped up to the front of the stage as Gus walked off to the side.

"Those of you who've been following us for years have heard this before, so bear with me while I fill everyone else in." He looked down at his guitar as he tuned it then back at the crowd. "More years ago than I care to admit, this was my senior prom song. I was lucky enough to be dating the most beautiful girl in the school at the time and she agreed to be my date. Five years later, we played this same song at our wedding for our first dance as husband and wife. Thirty-six years later it's still my favorite song and she's still my favorite girl." He looked over at Keera's mom and held up his pick. "This one's for you, El."

I stepped up behind Keera and wrapped my arms around her waist. She leaned against me with her hands over mine and we swayed to the music as we listened to her father sing "Just Between You and Me" by April Wine.

As the song ended, I turned Keera in the circle of my arms and gave her a kiss.

"We don't have a song," I said. "I think we need to get one."

She smiled.

"It's not that easy, you know. You can't just pick one randomly. It needs to be an organic thing."

"We'll have to work on it."

As the band sped things up again, I decided it was time

to hit the bathroom. I've been holding it for at least four songs, figuring they'd finish playing soon, but since that didn't happen, I'm going to have to brave the crowd.

"I'm gonna head to the bathroom," I said against Keera's ear.

She nodded and I turned around and meandered through people until I found the men's room. As I closed the door, I appreciated the lower decibel level inside. I'm really enjoying myself, but we're standing right near the speakers and it's *loud*.

The bathroom is closer to the bar and I decided to get a Coke before heading back to the group. I texted Keera and asked if she or anyone else wanted anything. When she texted back saying everyone was good, I headed out and crashed into Zoe.

"I'm sorry," she said.

"Sorry about that," I said at the same time and instinctively reached out to steady her.

Jill stopped at the entrance to the ladies' room with the door open and Zoe waved at her to go inside.

"I'm glad I bumped into you," she said, then chuckled and added. "Literally." Leaning closer, she continued. "After listening to you talk about Keera for years, I'm glad I finally got to know her. She's really amazing and you two are adorable together."

I had no idea what to say to that so I just nodded.

"You look happy," she said.

"I am."

"Good. You're a great guy, you deserve to be."

"Thanks."

I have no idea what Zoe's love life looks like these days and it's really none of my business. Before things turned awkward, Jill stepped out of the bathroom.

"I'm heading to the bar. Do either of you want anything?"

"Oh thanks, you're saving me a trip," Zoe said. "I'd love a white wine."

"Same," Jill said when I looked at her.

"Two white wines coming up," I said then walked over to the bar.

I got the drinks then chuckled to myself as I made my way toward the front holding two wine glasses in one hand and my soda in the other. I've never been a waiter, but might just have a knack for it.

As I reached my group, I held out my hand so Jill and Zoe could take their drinks. Making my way next to Keera, I asked if she wanted a sip of my soda. She looked at me out of the corner of her eye and shook her head.

The band played three more songs before finishing with what Gus called their *favorite one-hit wonder and namesake*, "Afternoon Delight" by the Starland Vocal Band.

When I jokingly suggested that be our song, Keera rolled her eyes and shook her head.

After the band finished, the crowd thinned a little bit. Keera's "pole peeps" left when the music stopped, deciding to hit a nightclub a few blocks away. We opted to stay and hang out with our parents instead.

Before sitting at the table, Keera and Anjannette headed to the ladies' room. I sat next to Archer who was talking to my mom. Andrew was across from me.

"What do you know about Zoe's friend Sacha?"

He rested his elbow on the table and leaned in as he spoke.

"Not a lot. They work together. I've been in her company a few times and she seems nice." I shrugged. "Why? You interested?"

"Maybe. I don't know. We were talking and I got her number." He finished his beer in one long chug. "I was just wondering if you had any inside intel."

"Nope. Sorry."

Archer had shifted to follow our conversation.

"You know, when I saw Zoe here tonight, I thought it was going to be bad," he said. "But she didn't get on my nerves like she used to and Keera didn't seem bothered."

"There's no reason she should be bothered," I said, glancing at Keera's parents to see if they were listening.

Archer snorted.

"I don't claim to know women, but common sense tells me that's flawed thinking on your part."

CHAPTER 29

Keera

I TURNED FROM SIDE TO SIDE, LOOKING AT MYSELF IN THE mirror from every angle and don't like what I see.

"What's that face for?" Anjannette asked.

"What was I thinking with this outfit?"

She looked at my reflection.

"Why? It looks great."

When I first saw these pole shorts, I fell in love with them. The high waisted booty short seemed like the perfect style to cover my stomach and show off my butt. I have to admit the halter top with its mesh insert makes the girls look amazing, but there's a roll of fat right under the band on my back.

"I must have gained weight since I tried these on."

"That's not true, but even if you did, that was just three weeks ago. How much could you have gained?"

"You'd be surprised. Weight sticks to me like I'm Velcro."

I turned around and looked at my back. "Seriously, look at that."

She walked over and adjusted my top.

"It was sitting in a weird place. What do you think now?"

I scrunched my nose.

"It's a little better, but I'm still not loving it." I reached for my duffel bag. "Maybe I have a tank top I can wear."

"You are *not* covering up," she said. "You look amazing."

"I look huge."

"No you don't." She put her hands on her hips. "What's this about?"

I shook my head and fussed with my pole shorts, trying to get them to cover more.

"I can't let Simon see me in this."

"Keera, the man has seen you naked."

"That's probably better than this. At least every roll isn't highlighted by dark material."

"Well I'm sorry, this show has a strict PG-13 rating. I can't let you go out there naked."

I know she's trying to make me laugh, but I'm just not feeling it. Instead I offered a small smile.

After scrutinizing myself in the mirror again, I reached for my silky robe and shrugged as I slipped it over my shoulders.

"I guess it is what it is at this point."

"Hey, perk up. You're the opening act and you're going to kill it." She put her arm around my shoulders and squeezed. "Come on. It's standing room only out there and it's almost time to get started."

We walked out of our small office and into the dressing room where our students were scrambling to get ready.

"Can I have a minute?" Anjannette yelled over the nervous din in the room. "You ladies have all worked so hard getting ready for tonight and I know you're going to be amazing out there. So relax and enjoy this moment. You're badass bitches and I love you all."

Everyone laughed at that last comment then looked at me.

"Everyone in that studio is here to cheer you on and celebrate your accomplishments. Just go out there and have fun. You've earned it."

We walked across the hall but before Anjannette went into the studio, she gave me another quick hug.

"I hope you take your own advice. You look absolutely beautiful and you're going to be great out there."

I stayed in the doorway as she walked into the studio to get the audience seated and make some opening remarks. People scrambled to their chairs and I looked around the room and spotted my parents first and saw Simon, Shannon, Andrew, Archer, and Leo sitting next to them. I returned Simon's wave but my smile froze on my face when I noticed Zoe right behind him. She leaned forward and said something to him and he nodded.

Closing my eyes, I took in a deep breath and fought to get into a dancing mindset. I'd just hung my robe up on the coat rack when I heard Anjannette's voice, but didn't pay close enough attention to understand her words. But I knew I was up when the first slow strains of "Criminal" by Fiona Apple echoed through the studio.

Thankfully, my dance doesn't officially start until Fiona actually starts singing, so I had time to slowly walk to the pole. As I started to dance, everything else faded away and I just let my body move to the music.

SIMON

THIS WHOLE SHOW HAS BEEN ABSOLUTELY AMAZING. Obviously I came to see Keera, but each and every performance has blown my mind.

Next up is the intermediate group led by Keera and Anjannette. They're dancing to "Circus" by Britney Spears and each have on a mask depicting an animal. Keera is a lion and looks sexy as hell in a tan outfit with her long brown hair curled and flowing around her shoulders.

There was a lot going on during the dance, but I kept my eyes firmly focused on Keera. I clapped along with the rest of the audience as I watched one incredible trick after another. Half the time I had no idea how the dancers stayed on the pole. And other times, I thought for sure they were going to crash to the ground, but thankfully that never happened.

I watched Keera climb to the top of the pole and settle into what she told me is called a pole sit. Phoebe did the same thing on the pole across from her and Anjannette stepped in between them and reached up, grabbing onto their outstretched hands. My jaw hit the floor when Anjannette flipped forward then backward before going forward again and landing in a split. I looked around and saw the other dancers were doing the same acrobatics.

Shannon bumped me with her shoulder.

"Are you watching this?" When I didn't answer quickly enough, she punched me in the arm. "Seriously, are you seeing this?"

"Yes, I'm seeing it." I rubbed my arm. "Stop hitting me."

She laughed then let out a catcall and clapped harder.

As the song came to an end, the dancers moved through

the poles, circling around each other. On the final note, they each grabbed onto the nearest pole, held on, and rotated down to the floor.

As the audience clapped, the dancers took a quick bow, then everyone but Anjannette left the floor. She's doing the last dance of the night.

I watched her slower, more artistic routine, but I'll be honest, in my mind, I mentally replayed Keera's time on the floor. One thing I know for sure is that when I buy a house, I need to make sure there's space for a pole.

THE AFTER PARTY TOOK UP THE WHOLE BACK HALF OF POOR Richard's Pub. We pushed a bunch of tables together and basically made the space our own. Keera sat on one side of me and Archer was on the other. He was leaning over me as he talked to her about the physics of pole dance.

"I have no idea how it works, I just know how to do it," she said.

"Would you mind if Simon shares the video of your dance with me so I can upload it to my computer and break it down mechanically?"

Keera looked at me and I shrugged.

"Sure. You can do that," she said. "Maybe you'll be able to help me do a rainbow."

"What's that?" he asked.

She picked up her cell and Googled it then handed it to him. He watched it three times before handing her phone back to her.

"I have no idea if it will help you, but I can break down the physics."

Anjannette and Leo were sitting across from us and they

joined in the discussion. Archer was in his element, talking physics when Zoe and Sacha approached.

"Is anyone sitting here?" Sacha asked Anjannette.

"No. Have a seat."

Sacha sat right across from Andrew and they each leaned forward, starting their own conversation leaving Zoe on her own.

"The show was incredible," she said, directing the comment to both Anjannette and Keera. "I hope to keep taking classes after the beginner's series is over." Gesturing toward Sacha, she added, "I'm so glad she asked me to go along with her."

"You've been doing great," Anjannette said.

"I'm just glad I was finally able to climb to the top of that damn pole. Thanks to Keera."

"Hey, that was all you. The only thing I did was cheer you on."

"I can't believe there are only two more classes. It went by so fast."

"Next class we're going to give you information on regular class packages," Anjannette said. "We're offering some one-time specials if you sign up after the series."

"One question, do you have to do the beginners' series to take classes?"

"No, you can just go to a beginner class, but the series helps you learn basic moves and tricks in a certain time-frame," Keera said. "We change things up in the beginner classes, so there are some things you might not learn immediately."

"I asked because my cousin might be interested in coming with me." She looked at me. "Joannie, believe it or not."

"Does she know that she won't be able to wear slacks and a silk blouse to class?"

Zoe laughed.

"I showed her pictures of what I've been doing in class so she should have a clue." She shrugged. "I'm not going to discourage her if she wants to come along. It's so much fun and it's such a great workout. And you know how much I hate exercise."

That led to a funny discussion about different things she's done through the years. Anjannette commented on P90-X, calling it torture. Leo joined in after that, talking about the yoga classes he takes from Clay, the man who owns the building the pole studio is in.

"I thought I was going to die during the first few classes," he said. "Literally. And now that I've been doing it for a year, I still feel that way sometimes."

"Remember when I took yoga, Simon?" Zoe asked. "I couldn't move the next day."

"I totally understand," Leo said.

As the conversation continued, I looked at Keera, who seemed to be following along, but looked a little pale under the makeup she was still wearing. I put my arm on the back of her chair and leaned closer.

"Are you feeling okay?"

"Yeah, just tired." She offered a weak smile. "I think it's just the letdown now that this is all over."

"Now that it is, you'll be able to relax a little." I kissed her forehead. "I know I'm looking forward to seeing you more often."

"Yeah, both of those things sound great."

CHAPTER 30

Keera

I PICKED THE NAIL POLISH OFF MY THUMB AND TRIED TO GET my thoughts together. I've been thinking about this since Simon dropped me off on Saturday night. It's three days later and I still don't know what to say to Dr. Green.

We've been here before. There were times when I first started seeing her that we sat in silence for at least part of the hour. Which is really stupid on my part. I can sit quietly anywhere else for free.

Looking up at the ceiling, I took in a deep breath then let it out slowly before finally speaking.

"I've told you about my insecurities with Simon when his ex-girlfriend is near." She nodded, but remained silent, her pen poised over her notebook. "I understand this is a *me* issue. He hasn't done anything. So in reality, there's *nothing* wrong." I dragged my fingers through my hair and shook my head. "But there is."

"Have you talked to Simon about this?"

"What am I going to say? I'm projecting my ex-boyfriend's actions onto you? I'll sound insane."

"Maybe he can help alleviate your insecurities. Or help you work through them."

"I don't see how talking to him will do anything but make me look ridiculous."

"Why do you think that?"

"Because I am being ridiculous," I said. "Simon is sweet and in my mind, I *know* he's not like Brian. And I'm as certain as I can be that he'd never do the kind of things Brian did. Or Jason. Or any of the others." I stood and paced behind the chair I'd just vacated. "But feelings aren't logical. I've been teaching Zoe pole dance for the past several weeks and we've gotten along fine. But when she's in a room with Simon, that changes. All the insecurities I had during my past relationships come rushing back when they interact in any way. Including my old body issues."

I waited until she finished writing before continuing.

"Zoe came to see my dad's band play and at one point, I saw Simon talking to her. That old feeling of dread washed over me. Then a week later, a bunch of us went out after the pole recital and Zoe ended up sitting across from us. She was saying lovely things about Anjannette and me and the classes she's taken and I faked my way through the whole conversation."

"In what way?"

I flopped back into the chair and crossed my legs.

"I just wanted to get out of there, get Simon out of there." I shook my head. "And the thing is, Zoe is just an easy scapegoat for my feelings. If I'm being honest, a diluted form of them is around when he interacts with other women too. But that's more random. With Zoe, it's every time."

"You've admitted yourself that this relationship is relatively new." I nodded. "You've also said that you and Simon have said that you love each other."

"Yeah, we have."

"And you truly believe you're in love, despite the short time you've been together."

"I do. Remember that we were friends first so I think that speeds things up a little."

"Okay, so he loves you and you love him. Tell me what more you want."

It only took me a second to figure out how to explain what I want out of my relationship. She listened as I relayed what my father said before singing last week.

"My dad has played in his band for forty years. Even local bands have groupies. I've seen women hit on him when he comes off stage. I asked my mom once if she gets worried or jealous when my dad plays, especially when she's not with him. Without hesitation, she told me that she trusts my dad. *That's* what I want."

"You said that you don't think Simon would cheat, so what are you worried about?"

"I'm worried that how I let guys treat me in the past has fucked me up too much and I'll never have a normal relationship. That I'll never truly trust anyone I'm involved with. Simon deserves a partner who loves him unconditionally and trusts him implicitly. He shouldn't have to walk around on eggshells every time he's around a female because I've been scarred by ex-boyfriends." I wiped a tear from my cheek and looked over at her. "Maybe I still need some time to work through all this before Simon and I move forward."

I raised my voice at the end of that sentence turning it into a question.

"I stand by my original advice. Talk to Simon."

Simon

I STOPPED AT THE JEWELRY STORE AFTER WORK TO PICK UP Keera's Christmas present. When my dad mentioned my grandmother's ring at Thanksgiving, I came up with the idea of what to get her. If I have my way, she'll have said ring someday, so I decided to gift her a matching bracelet.

There are enough pictures of the ring in our family photo albums, so I didn't have to ask my dad to retrieve it from the safe deposit box. The jeweler was able to create a beautiful design from the photo and I'm itching to see how it turned out.

The bell over the door rang as I entered the store and I spotted the owner sitting behind the counter. Lucas and his wife Jane opened this place thirty years ago and my dad has been buying jewelry for my mom here that entire time, including her engagement ring.

"Simon. How are you?"

Lucas removed his magnifying glasses and set them on the table as he stood.

"I'm good." I shook his hand then rested my hands on the counter. "Jane called earlier
and said my bracelet is ready."

"Yes, it is," he said. "Let me go get it."

He returned a few minutes later with a green, velvet box in hand. After setting it on the counter in front of me, he opened it, adding a little flair to the action. I picked up the bracelet and studied the design as it draped over my hand.

With its Celtic knots, scroll details, and shamrock motif in the white gold band, my grandmother's ring has a decidedly Gaelic design. There's a heart detailing in the setting, that holds up a nearly perfect round stone. Jane managed to incorporate all those elements into the design of the bracelet.

"It's perfect," I said, then took one last look before placing it back in the box. "What's my balance?"

He rattled off the number and I handed him my credit card. It's definitely more than I've ever spent on a Christmas present, but hopefully this will be a family heirloom someday. After signing the receipt, I took the small bag Lucas had placed the bracelet in.

"Tell Jane I said thank you and Merry Christmas if I don't see you."

"I'll definitely tell her and Merry Christmas to you, too."

I got back in the car and reached over to place the bag in my glove compartment. Keera and I are going to order takeout and watch a movie. Granny Vi's house isn't too far from the jewelry store, so I was standing outside her door in no time. Keera opened it, looking adorable in black leggings and an oversized Peaches & Pole sweatshirt.

"Hi," she said and stepped back so I could enter.

"Hi." I leaned down and kissed her. "Your tree looks nice," I said.

"Thanks." She sighed. "I love Christmas, but it's coming too fast. I'm not ready."

"Yeah, that seems to happen every year. It seems to come faster and faster."

I followed Keera's lead and settled onto the couch.

"The food should be here any minute. I ordered it about a half hour ago."

"What'd you decide on?"

"I had a craving for pad Thai."

"Sounds good," I said then looked around. "Is Granny Vi here?"

"No, she's gone out with Izzy."

I shifted closer to Keera, but the doorbell sounded before I could kiss her. She looked at me with wide eyes then stood to go answer the door.

"What do you want to drink?" she asked as she set the bag down on the coffee table.

"Water is fine."

She returned with two bottles and handed one to me then sat on the other side of the couch, curling her legs onto the cushion between us. I reached into the bag and handed her a container.

"Chopsticks or fork?" I asked.

"Chopsticks."

I handed her a set then grabbed one for myself along with my food and sat back.

An old episode of *Friends* was on and we watched while we ate. For a few minutes anyway.

"Simon, I want to talk to you about something."

"Okay." I set my chopsticks on top of the container. "What's up?"

"Something I discussed with Dr. Green on Tuesday."

As she toyed with her food, I stayed silent and waited for her to speak. It seemed to take forever, but she finally did. And at first what she said didn't seem so serious, but as she continued, it became more obvious that it is. To her anyway.

I've been on the other end of an "it's not you, it's me" speech before, and it kind of sounds like that's what this is.

"Keera, it's natural to be a little jealous, don't you think?"

After I asked that, I realized what a stupid question it is. If she didn't think so, we wouldn't be having this conversation.

"It's not exactly jealousy I feel. It's..." She trailed off then shifted forward to set her container on the table. "It's more than that. And none of what I'm feeling has anything to do with you or something you've done. You're perfect. I'm the one who's screwed up."

I shifted forward and reached for her but she pressed back against the arm of the couch. I'd be lying if I said her rebuff didn't sting.

"You're not screwed up."

"I don't know what else to call it. I have issues because of things that have happened in my past. You deserve someone who doesn't mentally freak out every time you're in the company of other women."

She took my hand in hers and squeezed.

"Remember when I was upset when I found out that you and Zoe still talk?"

"Yeah."

"You told me that you didn't have a bad breakup." I nodded. "I've never *not* had a bad breakup. I also haven't had a normal relationship. There was always some kind of drama or issue. That's one reason I enjoy being with you so much. It's fun and easy."

"Yes it is," I said. "And I think we can work through anything."

She shook her head.

"Based on things I've said through the years, I'm sure you already figured out that Brian cheated on me. I won't make you listen to all the crappy details, but what it boils down to is that he cheated on me. A lot. One of the women was his ex, which is why that's a trigger."

"Keera, I'm not Brian. I'd *never* cheat on you."

She offered a sad smile then let my hand go.

"I know that. I swear to you that deep in my heart, I know that." She swallowed and blinked back tears. "But there's some warped place deep inside me that's just reactive. And it triggers my insecurities about our relationship *and* my body issues."

She took a drink of water then set the bottle back on the coffee table.

"This issue was there after I found out you and Zoe are still friends. But I bumped into Brian a couple weeks ago and a lot of my insecurities were brought to the forefront."

"Was that when you kept saying you were tired?" She nodded. "I *knew* something was wrong. What did he say?"

"It doesn't matter." She shook her head. "What does is the fact that he could affect me at all. If I was truly over everything, that wouldn't happen."

She seemed so sad and so determined to let this affect our relationship.

"Keera, none of this matters," I said. "I love you and you love me. *That's* what matters."

"I wish it was that easy."

"It is if you let it be."

She shook her head and looked down at her hands.

I have no idea what to say, how to convince her that I'm perfectly happy with our relationship. If she gets jealous or whatever, we can deal with that as it comes along.

"So what do you think we should do?"

She took in a deep breath and let it out before looking me in the eye.

"I think we should take a break."

"A break?" She nodded. "For how long?"

"I'm not sure."

"Keera, don't do this. Please don't let Brian and whoever else ruin the good that's between us."

"I love you Simon. I really do." A tear escaped her eye and rolled down her cheek and she wiped it away. "Please give me some time to deal with this."

"Do I have a choice?"

CHAPTER 31

Keera

"You look like shit."

"Gee, thanks Anjannette." I set my bag down on the floor then flopped onto the chair. "A lady always likes to be complimented."

She rolled the desk chair over and rested her feet on the arm of the couch.

"You're here early."

"I had to get out of the house. Granny Vi's hostile stares and sarcastic comments are starting to get to me," I said. "I wasn't expecting you to be here."

"I met with Clay to sign the lease paperwork. We're officially here for another three years."

"That's great."

"Yeah, you sound thrilled."

I admit my words sounded less-than enthusiastic, but I really am happy about it.

"No, it's great. I'm just…" I trailed off and gestured with my hand, hoping that would end the sentence for me.

"It's been a week since you've seen or talked to Simon. Are you ready to call him?"

I shook my head and blinked to keep the ever-present tears at bay.

"What for? Nothing would be different."

"I don't know why you think something would have to be. You guys love each other and are perfect together. Why are you complicating it?"

"Seriously Anjannette? You of all people are asking me why I'm complicating my relationship?"

Her eyes rounded and she dramatically pressed her hand against her chest.

"What did I do?"

"Is your memory that short? Or do you really not remember breaking up with Leo over an issue very similar to mine."

"That's all the more reason for you to listen to me. I almost lost Leo because I was being ridiculous. You should take heed and learn from my mistakes."

"*Take heed*?"

I laughed for the first time in over a week over her choice of words.

"I thought it added a nice touch." She shrugged. "Plus it's something you should definitely do."

"And *you* should understand my feelings more than anyone." I took in a shuddering breath. "I don't want to feel this way and I don't want to hurt Simon."

Anjannette dropped her feet to the floor, rested her elbows against her knees, and leaned closer to me.

"Keera, the reason I broke up with Leo is because I was afraid of losing myself again, like I did with every other guy in my past. But he didn't want that any more than I did. You know why?" I shook my head. "Because he's a decent, sweet, amazing man who wants a real partner, not someone who's going to morph themselves into a reflection of him. He's secure enough in *himself* to let me be myself, which is what was missing in all the other guys I dated."

I shifted my gaze away from her and focused on the wall at the far end of the room. What she's saying makes sense, but no amount of logic is going to change how I feel.

"You know that I get caught up in my head sometimes. And trust me when I tell you that sitting in the stands watching groupies offer themselves to my boyfriend triggered each and every one of my insecurities. But instead of letting those negative thoughts and feelings take hold, Leo and I talked about them and moved forward." She reached out and squeezed my knee. "Simon is a great guy and I have no doubt that together, you can work through anything. You just need to give him the chance."

I swiped at my cheeks as I heard voices out in the hall. Time to put on my game face and give the class my best. I'll have to think about everything Anjannette said later.

SIMON

I walked into the house and headed toward the stairs to go straight to my room. It's been a long day and I'm too tired to put on a happy front for my family.

"Simon? Is that you?" my mom yelled.

So close.

"Yeah."

I reversed direction and walked into the kitchen where I found her sitting at the island writing on the notepad in front of her. She looked up at me and frowned.

"Is everything okay?"

I nodded and set my backpack on the floor.

"I'm just tired."

She didn't seem convinced, but didn't push either.

"Do you know what you and Keera are doing for the holidays?"

I haven't told anyone that Keera and I are taking a *break*. At first I didn't expect it to last this long and now I just don't want to talk about it.

"No, I don't."

"We can work around her family if you're going to both houses like you did at Thanksgiving. I just need to know so I can plan a time."

"Just plan it whenever and we'll make it work."

She carefully placed her pen next to her notebook then folded her hands and rested them under her chin.

"What's going on Simon?"

Her tone of voice made me feel like a guilty adolescent.

"Nothing."

"I know when something is bothering my children. And there's definitely something going on with you the past week. So spill."

I really don't want to talk about this, but I know she won't quit so I might as well get it over with.

"Keera and I are taking a break."

She blinked then raised her eyebrows.

"I thought everything was going well with the two of you."

"Me too," I said then added, "but she's working through some things."

"And you can't do that together?"

I shrugged.

"Apparently not."

"I saw Zoe at the concert. Did something happen with her?"

"*No.* I'd never cheat on Keera."

"I didn't think so but I had to ask just to rule it out," she said. "So what's going on?"

I don't want to offer any specifics. My mom wouldn't judge or tell anyone, but Keera's issues are hers to share. I thought for a minute, trying to figure out how to tell my mom what's happening without actually *telling* her.

"Nothing that happened between us," I said. "But there are some things from her past she's working through."

She rested her elbow against the island and shifted her whole body to face me.

"Did I ever tell you about the time I broke up with your father?"

"No. Why?"

"You know our basic story. He was the star athlete in high school and I was the nerd who tutored him in science senior year so he didn't become academically ineligible. Then to everyone's shock...including my own...he asked me to the prom. He'd been flirting with me for months at that point, but I *never* thought he was serious.

"We started dating after that and were inseparable all summer before leaving for college. I felt like I was living in my own true-life version of *Sixteen Candles*. The guy every girl wanted chose me and I was on cloud nine. Then we had to leave for college. Our schools were only two hours apart, but I had work and my course load, and he had football so we didn't have a lot of weekends together. I made it a point to go to some of his home games, and when I was there, a seed of insecurity got planted that just grew until it consumed me. I imagined all kinds of things." She shook her head. "When we were home for Christmas break, I told him I didn't want to see him anymore. He was confused, and for good reason."

"This is the first I'm hearing of this, so I'm guessing you weren't apart long."

"Two weeks," she said. "But it felt like forever."

"So how'd you get back together?"

"Remember this is pre cell phones and internet. The only way for him to get hold of me was to call the landline or come to the house."

"So what did he do?"

"Both. Repeatedly. My mother got sick of it, and when he showed up at the house one day, she brought him to my room and insisted I talk to him." She smiled. "Once I shared what was going on in my head, we were able to work through it. Because, in the big picture, it wasn't a big issue."

"I already know what's going on in Keera's head."

"Then that's half the battle," she said. "Go see her. Talk to her."

"She said she wanted a break."

She stood and wrapped her arms around my shoulder and squeezed before pulling back to look me in the eye.

"And *I* told your father I didn't want to see him again."

CHAPTER 32

Keera

I curled up on the couch with my favorite cozy blanket and turned on *The Office*. Normally I'd put on the *Gilmore Girls* when I'm feeling low, but I was with Simon the last time I watched it, so it would only make me feel worse.

Granny Vi came downstairs and stood between the TV and me.

"I'm going out with June," she said. "Darren and Cole are in for the holiday and they're taking us out to dinner tonight."

"Have fun."

"Are you just going to lay on that couch and wallow for the entire holiday season?"

"I don't know what I'm going to do," I said.

"The way I see it, what you're doing is messing up things with a good guy."

"Granny Vi, please."

"Please what? I've never pulled punches with you and I'm not going to now," she said. "I once told you that you needed to find a man who recognizes that you're the best thing in the world. I knew the minute I saw you two together that Simon Parker is that man. And I have no idea why you're letting every putz you dated ruin what the two of you have."

"It's more complicated than that."

"It's really not."

She just looked at me for several heartbeats before her face and voice softened.

"Life is too short to push away the people who love you, Keera."

After dropping that bomb, she picked up her coat and walked out the door.

I know that Simon is the best thing that ever happened to me. My fear has always been that I'm not good for him. But I suppose I should have enough faith in him to make that decision.

Picking up my phone, I clicked on Simon's name. I typed and deleted four different messages before settling on something simple.

Can we talk?

My stomach flipped when the three dots appeared almost immediately. I held my breath until I read his response.

.   .   .

Sure.

THE DOORBELL RANG JUST AS I WAS ABOUT TO TEXT HIM BACK to make a plan to get together. Tossing off my blanket, I walked over to the door and peeked through the window. My heart skipped a beat then did its best to pound out of my chest when I saw Simon standing there smiling at me.

I fumbled to unlock the door, then pulled it open with such force, it slammed against the wall. Acting on instinct, I wrapped my arms around Simon's neck and slammed up against him.

"I missed you so much," I whispered against his neck.

SIMON

I CAUGHT KEERA AND HELD HER TIGHT AGAINST ME. IT'S COLD out, but there's no way I'll interrupt this moment just to get warm. If I had my way, I'd never let her go.

She pulled back just enough to give me a quick kiss.

"How did you get here so fast? I *just* texted you."

"I was sitting outside in my car when I got your text."

"You were?" The corner of her mouth kicked up into an adorable smile. "Why?"

"Because I couldn't stand not being with you for another second."

Loosening her hold on my neck, she put some space between our bodies allowing the cold air in.

"Let's get inside," she said as she backed up.

I stepped inside, thankful for the warmth, and she

closed the door behind me. Taking my hand, she led me to the couch and we settled in next to each other. She reclined against the armrest and draped her legs over my thighs. I shifted to look her in the eye.

"Keera, I love you, and as long as you love me, I think we can work through anything."

"I do love you–"

Call me paranoid, but I was afraid those words were going to be followed by something I don't want to hear, so I interrupted.

"If there's a *but* coming after that, I'm seriously gonna cry."

She laughed at my words and reached out to stroke my cheek.

"Before you rudely interrupted me, I was going to say, I do love you *and* I agree. We *can* work through anything."

That's all I needed to hear at the moment. I shifted forward and opened my mouth over hers, taking it in a long, hard, deep kiss that hopefully showed her how much I love her and missed her.

When we finally came up for air, she smiled.

"Why don't we take this upstairs?"

I nodded and pressed back to stand and took her hand to pull her up. She led me up the stairs and to her room. The bedside lamp she turned on offered enough light so I could see every perfect inch I exposed as I slowly undressed her. I removed my own clothes in record speed and my erection nudged against her soft curves as we laid down in the middle of the bed.

Our hands caressed and mouths devoured so I was surprised when she pulled back and smiled at me.

"You know, I'm going to drive you crazy."

My own face split into a big smile as I imagined the word forever at the end of that sentence.

"I'd expect nothing less."

Her laugh turned to moans as I shifted on top of her and slipped inside.

EPILOGUE

Two months later

Simon unlocked the door and pushed it open. I went to step inside but he put his arm out to stop me.

"What's wrong?" I asked.

"I have to carry you over the threshold."

"That's the tradition after you get married," I said. "Besides, I'm too heavy."

He rested my hands against my waist and pulled me close for a kiss.

"You. Are. Perfect."

His image blurred when he said those words. Before I could respond, he bent down, placed his arm under my knees, and straightened, taking me with him. I held onto his neck as he stepped inside. After carrying me to the middle of the room, I slid down against his body as he slowly released me.

I kissed him, then pulled back and looked around.

"I can't believe this is our house."

"And I can't believe I get to spend the entire night with you."

"That's definitely a perk of homeownership."

Since Simon's parents decided not to hit the road again just yet, it took some innovation to get in sexy time. Neither Granny Vi or his parents would have blinked an eye if we'd slept together at their houses, but we both agreed we didn't want to do that.

As we walked through the empty rooms, I imagined how I'd decorate them. We bought some basic furniture, which will be delivered in the next week, but I want to take some time with the small touches that will make the house a home.

"This house is truly beyond perfect."

I looked around the kitchen, then out the patio doors. The pool is covered and the patio and yard have a light coating of snow, but I'm already picturing summer barbecues with friends and family.

"It definitely checked all our boxes and then some."

"I always loved Anjannette and Leo's house, but I never thought I'd have one just like it."

"This isn't quite as big as theirs."

"But it's the same design and in the same neighborhood."

He wrapped his arms around me and pulled me in for a kiss.

"I'm glad you like it."

"What about you?"

"I like whatever you like." He smiled. "You know what they say, 'happy wife, happy life.'"

I tilted my head to the side and raised my brow.

"I'm not your wife."

"No?"

I shook my head.

"Maybe we should do something about that."

My gasp echoed through the empty room when he stepped back, lowered to his right knee, and held up a black velvet box.

"Simon..." His name came out as both a whisper and a shriek.

"I'm pretty sure I fell in love with you the moment we met. But it wasn't our time yet and we became good friends. Thankfully our stars aligned and after ten years of friendship, we fell in love." He opened the box, exposing the most beautiful ring nestled inside. "Keera Jordan, will you marry me?"

I nodded and mouthed the word *yes* three times before finally saying it out loud. He slipped the ring on my finger then stood and placed his mouth over mine. The kiss was soft and sweet and sealed the new commitment we just made.

He pulled back and wiped tears from my cheeks.

"Why are you crying?"

"I'm just so happy." I shook my head. "Simon Parker, you're my person and I knew we'd be together forever. I wasn't expecting to get married, but I have to say, the thought makes me all mushy inside."

"And that's a good thing?"

"That's a very good thing." I held up my hand and looked down at my ring. Then shifted my eyes between it and the bracelet he gave me for Christmas. "Wait! Do these match?"

He nodded.

"My grandmother left me the ring and I knew you'd love it. So for Christmas, I went to my dad's favorite jewelry store and had them make a bracelet to match."

"So you knew you were going to propose at *Christmas*."

"Keera, I knew I wanted to propose the moment you agreed to go out with me." He flashed an adorable smile. "But I didn't want to come on too strong or seem too easy."

I wrapped my arms around his neck and kissed him.

"I love you, Simon Parker."

"I love you, too." He gave me another quick kiss then stepped back and pulled his phone out of his pocket. "Now that that's done, we have a group of people at Anjannette and Leo's house waiting to descend on us."

He texted and within minutes, our empty house was filled with family and friends, and every surface in the kitchen was covered with food. Simon's dad popped a bottle of champagne and poured it into plastic cups for a toast.

I looked around the room and my heart felt so full. This is everything I ever wanted but never thought I'd have.

Simon walked over and wiped a tear off my cheek.

"You're crying again."

"Get used to it. You're gonna have to deal with it for the rest of your life."

"It will be my pleasure."

The End

BOOK #2 OF THE PEACHES & POLE SERIES, GODDESS IN Training, is available for Preorder.

Check out Eve's story…

Chapter 1

Eve

I stared at the blinking cursor, praying for divine intervention to drop words into my head. Obviously not just any words. Wonderful words. Magical words. Or at least words my readers won't give a one-star review.

My cell vibrated, giving me a reason to tear my eyes away from the blank page. I smiled as my favorite aunt's face filled the screen.

"Aunt Winnie. How was the yoga retreat?"

"It was wonderful. The villa was absolutely beautiful and I felt such an amazing connection to all the attendees."

"I'm glad you enjoyed yourself."

"I truly did. There's nothing like getting away from your normal space. It really helps recenter and rejuvenate," she said.

"Your normal space is pretty great, but I suppose it still doesn't compare to Tuscany."

"Seaside is lovely but it's nice to visit other parts of the world from time to time. There's a different energy everywhere and it's so healthy to experience and absorb it."

Aunt Winnie is what my grandmother called *a hippy-dippy*. After graduating high school, she hopped into a Volkswagen Vanagon with five other people, hit the road, and lived like a nomad. She eventually settled in the idyllic town of Seaside, Oregon. And despite the fact she lived across the country from me, we managed to form a deep bond through her annual visits, phone calls, and a lot of letters.

"I should join you next time. A yoga retreat in Tuscany may be what I need to get myself straightened out."

"Oh honey, are you still having trouble writing?"

I nodded, even though she can't see.

"I've been a writer for the better part of a decade and yet, for the past three years, the words just won't come. It's like I forgot how to write. What's wrong with me?"

"You've experienced trauma and need to give yourself time to heal from that."

"The divorce was final three years ago. I should be healed by now."

"Hmmm, maybe," she said. "If you actually dealt with what happened."

"I think I dealt with it pretty well. As soon as I found out John was cheating, I told him I wanted a divorce. I even went back to using my maiden name once it was final. Not to mention how I stepped out of my comfort zone and started taking pole dance fitness classes. I'm in better shape than I was at eighteen. Plus I've made some amazing friends."

"That's all wonderful dear, but it doesn't mean you've mentally sorted through it all or let it go," she pointed out. "And the divorce isn't the only trauma you've experienced. Grace graduated college then moved to England to pursue her master's degree. That's a big change for a parent."

"I agree, the divorce and Grace moving across the pond were both big changes. But I honestly don't think either of those are my issue."

"Then what is?"

"I wish I knew."

Thankfully I had some books stockpiled so my publishing schedule hasn't totally

stopped, just slowed down a bit. But the last of my reserves is releasing next month, so if I don't write something else soon, I don't know what I'll do.

"I have an idea," Aunt Winnie said. "Why don't you come here for an extended visit?"

"I appreciate that, but I don't think I can."

"Why on Earth not?"

"I really need to get at least one book done and I don't write well on vacation."

"Everly, you haven't written well for the past three years and you haven't gone anywhere."

"Uh oh, using my full name. You must be serious."

"I am serious," she said. "A change of scenery might be just what you need. Plan on staying for the summer."

Honestly, there's no reason for me not to go. The only thing I'll be leaving behind is pole class. I'll miss my pole peeps, but it's only for a few months. If there's a chance it will help my words flow again, I'll take it. Plus it will be good to visit Aunt Winnie. We haven't seen each other in person since Grace's college graduation last year.

"Thanks Aunt Winnie. I'll book a flight and let you know when I'll be there."

Max

"Let me help you with that, Pop," I said. "Why didn't you wait for me?"

"I'm not an invalid. I've been unloading my own truck since before you were born."

Which is exactly why he shouldn't be doing it by himself. Instead of saying that and starting an argument, I emptied the last few items out of the truck. I watched my grandfather limp around to the passenger side and pull his toolbox out of the back seat.

"I can handle this if your gout is acting up."

"I'm fine," he grumbled. "Besides, this is a two-man job."

"It'll be easier with two, but I can handle it on my own if you need to rest."

"Ach, I'll rest when I'm dead."

It seems like he's pretty grumpy this morning so I let the subject drop. The man is seventy-three years old. He's not going to change his ways at this point.

I grabbed a hammer and pry bar out of my toolbox and walked over to start the demo. The small deck we're replacing is in pretty bad shape, so it didn't take too long to dismantle.

Pop stood off to the side and watched as I knocked down the rest of the deck. His foot must really be bothering him because he just stood off to the side watching instead of jumping in and showing me how to do it "the right way."

Once I had the whole thing torn apart, I tossed the old wood into the bed of my pickup and joined Pop over by the pile of new material.

"I hope this scheme of yours works. Otherwise we're gonna be in the hole on this job. My quotes don't leave enough room for us to spend double on material."

We usually cut all the material on site, but I suggested we start doing at least some of it in Pop's workshop and bring it with us instead. This is a small project, so it seemed like a good one to try my way. Surprisingly, he agreed without too much complaint.

"If it doesn't work, I'll pay for new material out of my own pocket."

"I forgot you have those Hollywood big bucks and don't have to worry about sticking to a budget."

Ignoring the jab, I picked up my toolbelt and snapped it into place. Pop generally isn't a ray of sunshine, but he's usually in a better mood than this. The best thing I can do is get to work and finish this job early so he can go home and rest.

We worked side by side and got the flooring and steps done in record time. Thankfully all the cut pieces fit with minimal tweaking.

"Let's take a break," I said. "I'm starving."

One thing I've learned through the years working with Pop is that he'll keep going until a job is done. But if I stop, he'll stop. So I make it a point to at least break for a drink to ensure he stays hydrated.

I ran to my truck and grabbed the cooler out of the back seat and joined Pop on the newly-constructed steps. Reaching inside, I handed him a bottle of water and a ham and cheese sandwich.

"Winnie Everly called last night. Her porch steps are loose and she needs a window in her studio replaced. Do you think you can handle that Saturday?"

That could explain some of his mood today, too. He and Winnie have been circling around each other since I moved here twelve years ago, and probably a couple decades before that too. I have no idea why they don't just get together. They're not getting any younger.

"Sure."

"I'd do it myself, but I have that meeting with the festival planning committee." He took a bite of his sandwich and chewed. "That shouldn't take too long though so maybe I can take care of Winnie's projects in the afternoon instead of having you do it."

"I don't have any plans for Saturday, so it's no problem."

"Guess I better take you up on that now because once the festival starts, you'll probably be busy." He grunted and shook his head. "You're thirty-three. Time to start settling down instead of just fooling around, don't you think?"

I'll admit that for the first few years I lived here, I was *very busy* during festival season. Vacationing women were perfect for what I was looking for at the time. Namely no-strings sex and for them to leave when it was over. And even though I haven't done that in a long time, Pop still brings it up every year.

The truth is, I'd settle down tomorrow if I found the right woman, but no one in Seaside fits that description. Maybe someday.